Sintram and His Companions

Friedrich de la Motte Fouqué (1777 – 1843) was a German writer of the romantic style. Although not originally intended for a military career, Fouqué gave up his university studies at Halle to join the army, however, the rest of his life was largely devoted to literary pursuits.

His trilogy of plays – *The Hero of the North* (1910), which included *Sigurd the Dragon Slayer*, *Sigurd's Revenge*, and *Aslauga* – was the first modern German dramatisation of the Nibelung legend. The trilogy brought Fouqué to the attention of the public, and had a considerable influence on subsequent versions of the story, such as Richard Wagner's *The Ring of the Nibelung*.

Fouqué's subsequent literary activity was divided between his interests of medieval chivalry and northern mythology. Between 1810 and 1815, Fouqué's popularity was at its peak, during which time *Undine*, the best known of Fouqué's considerable body of work, appeared. Fouqué has influenced many authors, including Robert Louis Stevenson, and his works are referred to in those such as Louisa May Alcott's *Little Women* and *Jo's Boys*.

Also by Friedrich de la Motte Fouqué

THE FOUR SEASONS Series

Sintram and His Companions: Winter

Undine, the Water Sprite: Spring

The Two Captains: Summer

Aslauga's Knight: Autumn

The Four Seasons: Sintram and His Companions, Undine, The Two Captains & Aslauga's Knight

THE FOUR SEASONS

Sintram and His Companions

WINTER

Story by Friedrich Heinrich Karl de la Motte
(Baron Fouqué)

Adapted by Rachel Louise Lawrence

Blackdown*Publications*

This edition of Friedrich de la Motte Fouqué's *"Sintram and His Companions"* from *'Undine and Other Tales'* (1867) first published in 2015 by Blackdown Publications

Blackdown*Publications*
Address 83 Blackdown View, Ilminster, Somerset TA19 0BD
Email blackdownpublications@mail.com

ISBN-13: 978-1518618819
ISBN-10: 1518618812

Illustration on front cover by Johan Christian Dahl (1827)

CONTENTS

INTRODUCTION

By Charlotte Mary Yonge

INTRODUCTION

These four tales are, it is said, intended by the Author to be appropriate to the Four Seasons: the stern, grave "Sintram", to winter; the tearful, smiling, fresh "Undine", to Spring; the torrid deserts of "The Two Captains", to summer; and the sunset gold of "Aslauga's Knight", to autumn.

The Author of these tales, as well as of many more, was Friedrich, Baron de la Motte Fouqué, one of the foremost of the minstrels or tale-tellers of the realm of spiritual chivalry – the realm to whatever place Arthur's knights departed when they "took the Sangreal's holy quest," – from the place Spenser's Red Cross knight and his fellows came forth on their adventures, and in which the Knight of la Mancha believed, and endeavoured to exist.

La Motte Fouqué derived his name and his title from the French Huguenot ancestry, who had fled on the Revocation of the Edict of Nantes. His Christian name was taken from his godfather, Frederick the Great, of whom his father was a faithful friend, without compromising his religious principles and practice.

Friedrich was born at Brandenburg on 12th February, 1777. Educated by good parents at home, he served in the Prussian army through disaster and success, took an enthusiastic part in the rising of his country against Napoleon, writing as many battle-songs as Korner.

When victory was achieved, he dedicated his sword in the church of Neunhausen, where his estate lay. He lived there, with his beloved wife and his imagination, until his death in 1843.

And all the time, life was to him a poet's dream. He lived in a continual glamour of spiritual romance, bathing everything, from the old deities of the Valhalla down to the champions of German liberation, in an ideal glow of purity and nobleness, earnestly Christian throughout, even in his dealings with Northern mythology, for he saw Christ unconsciously shown in Balder, and Satan in Loki.

Thus he lived, felt, and believed what he wrote, and though his dramas and poems do not rise above fair mediocrity, and the great number of his prose stories are injured by a certain monotony, the charm of them is in their elevation of sentiment and the earnest faith pervading all. His knights might be Sir Galahad – "My strength is as the strength of ten, / Because my heart is pure."

Evil comes to them as something to be conquered, generally as a form of magic enchantment, and his "wondrous fair maidens" are worthy of them. Yet there is adventure enough to afford much pleasure, and often we have a touch of true genius, which has given actual ideas to the world, and precious ones.

This genius is especially traceable in his two masterpieces, "Sintram" and "Undine". Sintram was inspired by Albert Durer's engraving of the "Knight of Death," of which we give a presentation. It was sent to Fouqué by his friend Edward Hitzig, with a request that he would compose a ballad on it. The date of the engraving is 1513, and we quote the description given by the late Rev. R. St. John Tyrwhitt, showing how differently it may be read.

"Some say it is the end of the strong wicked man, just overtaken by Death and Sin, whom he has served on earth. It is said that the tuft on the lance indicates his murderous character, being of such unusual size. You know the use of that appendage was to prevent blood running down from the spearhead to the hands. They also think that the object under the horse's off hind foot is a snare, into which the old oppressor is to fall instantly. The expression of the faces may be taken either way: both good men and bad may have hard, regular features; and both good men and bad would set their teeth grimly on seeing Death, with the sands of their life nearly run out. Some say they think the expression of Death gentle, or only admonitory (as the author of "Sintram"); and I have to thank the authoress of the "Heir of Redclyffe" for showing me a fine impression of the plate, where Death certainly had a not ungentle countenance—snakes and all. I think the shouldered lance, and quiet, firm seat on horseback, with gentle bearing on the curb-bit, indicate grave resolution in the rider, and that a robber knight would have his lance in rest; then there is the leafy crown on the horse's head; and the horse and dog move on so quietly, that I am inclined to hope the best for the Ritter."

Musing on the mysterious engraving, Fouque saw in it the life-long companions of man, Death and Sin, whom he must defy in order to reach salvation; and out of that contemplation rose his wonderful romance, not exactly an allegory, where every circumstance can be fitted with an appropriate meaning, but with the sense of the struggle of life, with external temptation and hereditary inclination pervading all, while Grace and Prayer aid the effort. Folko and Gabrielle are revived from the Magic Ring, that Folko may by example and influence enhance all higher resolutions; while Gabrielle, in all unconscious innocence, awakes the passions, and thus makes the conquest the harder."

It is within the bounds of possibility that the similarities of folklore may have brought to Fouqué's knowledge the outline of the story which Sir Walter Scott tells us was the germ of "Guy Mannering"; where a boy, whose horoscope had been drawn by an astrologer, as likely to encounter peculiar trials at certain intervals, actually had, in his twenty-first year, a sort of visible encounter with the Tempter, and came off conqueror by his strong faith in the Bible.

Scott, between reverence and realism, only took the earlier part of the story, but Fouqué gives us the positive struggle, and carries us along with the final victory and subsequent peace. His tale has had a remarkable power over the readers.

We cannot but mention two remarkable instances at either end of the scale. Cardinal Newman, in his younger days, was so much overcome by it that he hurried out into the garden to read it alone, and returned with traces of emotion in his face. And when Charles Lowder read it to his East End boys, their whole minds seemed engrossed by it, and they even called certain spots after the places mentioned. Imagine the Rocks of the Moon in Ratcliff Highway!

C. M. YONGE, 1896

SINTRAM AND HIS COMPANIONS

Winter

CHAPTER I

The Disturbance of Sintram

IN the high castle of Drontheim, many knights sat assembled to hold council for the state of the realm, and joyously they caroused together until midnight, around the huge stone table in the vaulted hall. A rising storm drove the snow wildly against the rattling windows; all the oak doors groaned, the massive locks shook, the castle clock slowly and heavily struck the hour of one.

Then a boy, pale as death, with disordered hair and closed eyes, rushed into the hall, uttering a wild scream of terror. He stopped beside the richly carved seat of the mighty Biorn, clung to the glittering knight with both his hands, and shrieked in a piercing voice, "Knight and father! Father and knight! Death and another are closely pursuing me!"

An awful stillness lay like ice on the whole assembly, save the boy screaming the ever-fearful words. But one of Biorn's numerous retainers, an old esquire, known by the name of Rolf the Good, advanced towards the terrified child, took him in his arms, and half chanted this prayer,

"Oh, Father, help your servant!
I believe, and yet I cannot believe."

The boy, as if in a dream, at once loosened his hold of the knight, and the good Rolf bore him from the hall unresisting, yet still shedding hot tears and murmuring confused sounds.

The lords and knights looked at one another, much amazed, until the mighty Biorn said, wildly and fiercely laughing, "Marvel not at that strange boy. He is my only son, and has been as you see him since he was five years old. He is now twelve. I am therefore accustomed to seeing him so, though, at first, I too was disquieted by it. The attack comes upon him only once in the year, and always at this same time. But forgive me for having spent so many words on my poor Sintram, and let us pass on to some worthier subject for our discourse."

Again, there was silence for a while; then whisperingly and doubtfully single voices strove to renew their broken-off discourse, but without success. Two of the youngest and most joyous began a roundelay[1], but the storm howled and raged so wildly outside that this too was soon interrupted. Now they all sat silent and motionless in the lofty hall; the lamp flickered sadly under the vaulted roof; the whole party of knights looked like pale lifeless images dressed up in gigantic armour.

Then arose the Chaplain of the castle of Drontheim, the only priest among the knightly throng and said, "Dear Lord Biorn, our eyes and thoughts have all been directed to you and your son in a wonderful manner, as if it has been ordered by the providence of God. You perceive that we cannot withdraw them, and you would do well to tell us exactly what you know concerning the fearful state of the boy. Perchance the solemn tale, which I expect from you, might be good for this disturbed assembly."

Biorn cast a look of displeasure on the priest, and answered, "Sir Chaplain, you have more share in the history than either you or I could desire. Excuse me, if I am unwilling to trouble these light-hearted warriors with so rueful a tale."

Heedless, the Chaplain approached nearer to the knight, and said, in a firm yet mild tone, "Dear lord, until this time it rested with you alone to relate it or not. Now that you have so strangely hinted at the share that I have had in your son's calamity, I must demand that you repeat, word for word, how everything happened. My honour will have it so, and that will weigh with you as much as with me."

In stern compliance Biorn bowed his haughty head, and began the following narration, "This time, seven years ago, I was keeping the Christmas feast with my assembled followers. We have many venerable old customs, which have descended to us by inheritance from our great forefathers – that of placing a gilded boar's head on the table, for instance, and making upon it knightly vows of daring and wondrous deeds. Our Chaplain here, who used then frequently to visit me, was never in favour of keeping up such traditions from the ancient heathen world, since men such as he were not looked upon with much favour in those olden times."

"My excellent predecessors," interrupted the Chaplain, "belonged more to God than to the world, and with Him they were in favour, to such a degree that they converted your ancestors, and if I can, in like manner, be of service to you, even your jeering will not vex me."

With looks yet darker, and a somewhat angry shudder, the knight resumed, "Yes, yes, I know all your promises and threats of an invisible Power, and how they are meant to persuade us to part more readily with whatever of this world's goods we may possess. Once, ah, truly, once I too had such! Strange! Sometimes it seems to me as though ages have passed over since then, and as if I were alone the survivor, so fearfully is everything changed. But now, I remind myself, that the greater part of this noble company knew me in my happiness, and have seen my wife, my lovely Verena."

He pressed his hands on his eyes, and it seemed as though he wept. The storm had ceased; the soft light of the moon shone through the windows, and her beams played on his wild features. Suddenly, he started up, so that his heavy armour rattled with a fearful sound, and he cried out in a thundering voice, "Shall I turn monk, as she has become a nun? No, crafty priest, your webs are too thin to catch flies of my sort."

"I have nothing to do with webs," said the Chaplain. "In all openness and sincerity, have I put Heaven and Hell before you during these last six years? Moreover, you gave full consent to the step that the holy Verena took. But what all that has to do with your son's sufferings, I know not, and I wait for your narration."

"You may wait long enough," said Biorn, with a sneer. "Sooner shall —"

"Swear not!" said the Chaplain in a loud, commanding tone, and his eyes flashed almost fearfully.

"Hurrah!" cried Biorn in wild terror. "Hurrah! Death and his companion are loose!" and he dashed madly out of the chamber and down the steps.

The rough and fearful notes of his horn were heard, summoning his retainers; and presently afterwards, the clatter of horses' feet on the frozen courtyard gave token of their departure.

The knights retired, silent and shuddering; while the Chaplain remained alone at the huge stone table, praying.

CHAPTER II

An Account of Christmas Past

AFTER some time the good Rolf returned with slow and soft steps, and started with surprise at finding the hall deserted; the chamber, where he had been occupied in quieting and soothing the unhappy child, was in so distant a part of the castle that he had not heard the knight's hasty departure.

The Chaplain related to him all that had passed, and then said, "But my good Rolf, I much wish to ask you concerning those strange words with which you seemed to lull poor Sintram to rest. They sounded like sacred words and, no doubt, they are, but I could not understand them. 'I believe, and yet I cannot believe.'"

"Reverend Sir," answered Rolf, "I remember that, from my earliest years, no history in the gospels has taken such hold of me than that of the child possessed with a devil, which the disciples were not able to cast out. However, when our Saviour came down from the mountain, where He had been transfigured, He broke the bonds by which the evil spirit had held the miserable child bound.

"I always felt as if I must have known and loved that boy, and been his playfellow in his happy days, and when I grew older, the distress of the father on account of his lunatic son lay heavy at my heart. It must surely have been a foreboding of our poor young Lord Sintram, whom I love as if he were my own child.

"Now, the words of the weeping father in the gospel often come into my mind, 'Lord, I believe; help Thou my unbelief', and something similar I may very likely have repeated today as a chant or a prayer.

"Reverend Father, when I consider how one dreadful curse of the father has kept its destructive hold on the son, all seems dark before me, but, God be praised, my faith and my hope remain aloft."

"Good Rolf," said the Chaplain, "I cannot clearly understand what you say about the unhappy Sintram, for I do not know when and how this affliction came upon him. If no oath or solemn promise bind you to secrecy, will you make known to me all that is connected with it?"

"Most willingly," replied Rolf. "I have long desired to have an opportunity of so doing, but you have been almost always separated from us. I dare not now leave the sleeping boy alone any longer, and tomorrow, at the earliest dawn, I must take him to his father. Will you come with me, dear sir, to our poor Sintram?"

The Chaplain at once took up the small lamp that Rolf had brought with him, and they set off together, through the long vaulted passages. In the small distant chamber, they found the poor boy fast asleep.

The light of the lamp fell strangely on his very pale face. The Chaplain stood gazing at him for some time, and at length said, "Certainly, from his birth his features were always sharp and strongly marked, but now they are almost fearfully so for such a child, and yet no one can help having a kindly feeling towards him, whether he wants or not."

"Most true, dear sir," answered Rolf, and it was evident how his whole heart rejoiced at any word that indicated affection for his beloved young lord. At that point, he placed the lamp where its light could not disturb the boy, and seating himself close by the priest, he began to speak.

"During that Christmas feast of which my lord was talking about to you, he and his followers conversed much concerning the German merchants, and the best means of keeping down the increasing pride and power of the trading towns. At length, Biorn laid his ungodly hand on the golden boar's head, and swore to put to death, without mercy, every German trader whom fate, in any way at all, might bring alive into his power.

"The gentle Verena turned pale, and would have interjected – but it was too late, the bloody word was uttered. Immediately afterwards, as though the great enemy of souls was determined to secure at once the vassal so devoted to him, a warder came into the hall and announced that two citizens of a trading town in Germany, an old man and his son, had been shipwrecked on this coast, and were now outside the gates, asking hospitality of the Lord of the Castle.

"The knight could not refrain from shuddering, but

he thought himself bound by his rash vow and by that accursed heathenish golden boar. We, his retainers, were commanded to assemble in the castle-yard, armed with sharp spears, which were to be hurled at the defenceless strangers at the first signal made to us.

"For the first, and I trust the last time in my life, I said, 'No' to the commands of my lord, and that I said in a loud voice, and with the heartiest determination. The Almighty, who alone knows whom He will accept and whom He will reject, armed me with resolution and strength. And, I suspect, Biorn perceived where the refusal of his faithful old servant arose, and that it was worthy of respect.

"He said to me, half in anger, half in scorn, 'Go up to my wife's apartments. Her attendants are running to and fro, perhaps she is ill. Go up, Rolf the Good, I say to you, and so women shall be with women.' I thought to myself, 'Jeer on, then,' and I went silently the way that he had pointed out to me.

"On the stairs, there I met two strange and fearful beings, whom I had never seen before and know not how they got into the castle. One of them was a great tall man, frightfully pallid and thin, the other was a dwarf-like man, with a most hideous countenance and features. Indeed, when I collected my thoughts and looked carefully at him, it appeared to me –"

Low moans and convulsive movements of the boy interrupted the narrative. Rolf and the Chaplain hastened to his bedside, and perceived that his countenance wore an expression of fearful agony, and that he was struggling, in vain, to open his eyes. The priest

9

made the Sign of the Cross over Sintram; peace immediately seemed to be restored, and his sleep became quiet once more. The two men both returned softly to their seats.

"You see," said Rolf, "that it will not do to describe more closely those two awful beings. Suffice to say, that they went down into the courtyard, and that I proceeded to my lady's apartments. I found the gentle Verena almost fainting with terror and overwhelming anxiety, and I hastened to restore her with some remedies, which I was able to apply by my skill, through God's gift and the healing virtues of herbs and minerals.

"But scarcely had she recovered her senses, when, with that calm holy power which, as you know, is hers, she desired me to conduct her down to the courtyard, saying that she must either put a stop to the fearful doings of this night, or she herself would become a sacrifice.

"Our way took us by the little bed of the sleeping Sintram. Hot tears fell from my eyes to see how evenly his gentle breath then came and went, and how sweetly he smiled in his peaceful slumbers." The old man put his hands to his eyes, and wept bitterly, but soon he resumed his sad story. "As we approached the lowest window of the staircase, we could hear distinctly the voice of the elder merchant. Moreover, on looking out, the light of the torches showed me his noble features, as well as the bright youthful countenance of his son.

"'I take Almighty God to witness,' cried he, 'that I had no evil thought against this house! Surely, I must have fallen unawares amongst heathens. It cannot be that

I am in a Christian knight's castle, and if you are indeed heathens, then kill us at once. And you, my beloved son, be patient and of good courage. In Heaven, we shall learn for which reason it could not be otherwise.'

"I thought I could see those two fearful ones amidst the throng of retainers. The pale one had a huge curved sword in his hand, the little one held a spear notched in a strange fashion. Verena tore open the window, and cried in silvery tones through the wild night, 'My dearest lord and husband, for the sake of your only child, have pity on those harmless men! Save them from death, and resist the temptation of the evil spirit.'

"The knight answered in his fierce wrath, but I cannot repeat his words. He staked his child on the desperate cast. He called on Death and the Devil to see that he kept his word – but hush! The boy is again moaning. Let me bring the dark tale quickly to a close. Biorn commanded his followers to strike, casting on them those fierce looks that have gained him the title of Biorn of the Fiery Eyes, while at the same time the two frightful strangers roused themselves, very busily.

"Then Verena called out, with piercing anguish, 'Help, oh God, my Saviour!' Those two dreadful figures disappeared, and the knight and his retainers, as if seized with blindness, rushed wildly one against the other, but without doing injury to themselves or being able to strike the merchants, who ran so close a risk.

"The merchants bowed reverently towards Verena, and with calm thanksgivings departed through the castle-gates, which at that moment had been burst open by a violent gust of wind, and now gave a free passage to any who would go forth.

"The lady and I still stood, bewildered, on the stairs, when I fancied I saw the two fearful forms glide close by me, mist-like and unreal. Verena called to me, 'Rolf, did you see a tall pale man, and a little hideous one with him, pass just now up the staircase?' I flew after them, and found the poor boy in the same state in which you saw him a few hours ago.

"Ever since, the attack has come on him regularly at this time and he is, in all respects, fearfully changed. The Lady of the Castle did not fail to discern the avenging hand of Heaven in this calamity. And as the knight, her husband, instead of repenting, became ever more truly Biorn of the Fiery Eyes, she resolved, in the walls of a cloister, by unremitting prayer, to obtain mercy in time and eternity for herself and her unhappy child."

Rolf was silent, and the Chaplain, after some thought, said, "I now understand why, six years ago, Biorn confessed his guilt to me in general words, and consented that his wife should take the veil. Some faint feeling of remorse or guilt must then have stirred within him, and perhaps may stir in him yet. At any rate, it was impossible that so tender a flower as Verena could remain anymore in so rough keeping. But who is there now to watch over and protect our poor Sintram?"

"The prayer of his mother," answered Rolf. "Reverend Sir, when the first dawn of day appears, as it does now, and when the morning breeze whispers through the glancing window, they ever bring to my mind the soft beaming eyes of my lady, and I again seem to hear the sweet tones of her voice. The holy Verena is, next to God, our chief aid."

"And let us add our devout supplications to the Lord," said the Chaplain; and he and Rolf knelt in silent and earnest prayer by the bed of the pale sufferer, who began to smile in his dreams.

CHAPTER III

Sintram Encounters a Pilgrim

THE rays of the sun shining brightly into the room awoke Sintram, and raising himself up, he looked angrily at the Chaplain, and said, "So there is a priest in the castle! Yet that accursed dream continues to torment me, even in his very presence. Pretty priest he must be!"

"My child," answered the Chaplain in the mildest tone, "I have prayed for you most fervently, and I shall never cease doing so, but God alone is Almighty."

"You speak very boldly to the son of the Knight Biorn," cried Sintram. "'My child!' If those horrible dreams had not again been haunting me, you would make me laugh heartily."

"Young Lord Sintram," said the Chaplain, "I am by no means surprised that you do not know me again, for in truth, neither do I know you again." And his eyes filled with tears as he spoke.

The good Rolf looked sorrowfully in the boy's face, saying, "Ah, my dear young master, you are so much better than you would make people believe. Why do you do that? Your memory is so good, that you must surely recollect your kind old friend the Chaplain, who formerly used to be constantly at the castle, and to bring you so many gifts – bright pictures of saints and beautiful songs?"

"I know all that very well," replied Sintram thoughtfully. "My sainted mother was alive in those days."

"Our gracious lady is still living, God be praised," said the good Rolf.

"But she does not live for us, poor sick creatures that we are!" cried Sintram. "And why do you not call her sainted? Surely she knows nothing about my dreams?"

"Yes, she does know of them," said the Chaplain, "and she prays to God for you. But take heed, and restrain that wild haughty temper of yours. It might, indeed, come to pass that she may know nothing about your dreams, and that would happen if your soul were separated from your body, and then the holy angels would also cease to know anything of you."

Sintram fell back on his bed, as if thunderstruck, and Rolf said, with a gentle sigh, "You should not speak so severely to my poor sick child, Reverend Sir."

The boy sat up and, with tearful eyes, he turned caressingly towards the Chaplain, "Let him do as he pleases, you good tender-hearted Rolf. He knows very well what he is about. Would you reprove him if I was slipping down a snow-cleft, and he caught me up roughly by the hair of my head?"

The priest looked tenderly at him, and would have spoken his holy thoughts, when Sintram suddenly sprang off the bed and asked after news of his father.

As soon as Sintram heard of the knight's departure, he would not remain another hour in the castle. He put aside the fears of the Chaplain and the old esquire, who were concerned a rapid journey would injure his hardly restored health, by saying to them, "Believe me, Reverend Sir, and dear old Rolf, if I were not subject to these hideous dreams, there would not be a bolder youth in the whole world. Even as it is, I am not so far behind the very best. Besides, 'til another year has passed, my dreams are at an end."

On his somewhat arrogant sign, Rolf brought out the horses. The boy threw himself boldly into the saddle, and taking a courteous leave of the Chaplain, he dashed along the frozen valley that lay between the snow-clad mountains.

He had not ridden far, in the company of his old attendant, when he heard a strange indistinct sound proceeding from a neighbouring cleft in the rock. It was partly like the clapper of a small mill, but mingled with that were hollow groans and other tones of distress. They turned their horses in that direction and a wonderful sight showed itself to them.

A tall man, deadly pale, in a pilgrim's garb, was striving with violent – though unsuccessful – efforts to work his way out of the snow and to climb up the mountain. As a consequence of his movement, a quantity of bones, which were hanging loosely all about his garments, rattled one against the other, and caused the mysterious sound.

Rolf, much terrified, crossed himself, while the bold Sintram called out to the stranger, "What are you doing there? Give an account of your solitary labours."

"I live in death," replied that other one with a fearful grin.

"Whose are those bones on your clothes?"

"They are relics, young sir."

"Are you a pilgrim?"

"Restless, I wander up and down."

"You must not perish here in the snow before my eyes."

"That I will not."

"You must come up and sit on my horse."

"That I will." And, all at once, he started up out of the snow, with surprising strength and agility, and sat on the horse behind Sintram, clasping him tight in his long arms.

Startled by the rattling of the bones, and as if seized with madness, the horse rushed away through the trackless passes.

The boy soon found himself alone with his strange companion; for Rolf, breathless with fear, spurred on his horse in vain, and remained far behind them.

From a snowy precipice the horse slid, without falling, into a narrow gorge, somewhat exhausted, yet continuing to snort and foam as before, and still not under the control of the boy. Yet with his headlong course changing into a rough irregular trot, Sintram was able to breathe more freely, and to begin the following discourse with his unknown companion.

"Draw your garment closer around you, pale man, so the bones will not rattle, and I shall be able to curb my horse."

"It would be of no avail, boy. It would be of no avail. The bones must rattle."

"Do not clasp me so tight with your long arms, they are so cold."

"It cannot be helped, boy. It cannot be helped. Be content, for my long cold arms are not pressing yet on your heart."

"Do not breathe on me so with your icy breath. All my strength is departing."

"I must breathe, boy. I must breathe. But do not complain. I am not blowing you away."

Here the strange dialogue ended; for, to Sintram's surprise, he found himself on an open plain, over which the sun was shining brightly, and at no great distance ahead of him, he saw his father's castle.

While he was thinking whether he would invite the unearthly pilgrim to rest there, the pale man put an end to Sintram's thoughts by throwing himself suddenly off the horse, whose wild course was checked by the shock.

Raising his forefinger, he said to the boy, "I know old Biorn of the Fiery Eyes well, perhaps too well. Commend me to him. You will not need to tell him my name. He will recognise me from your description."

So saying, the ghastly stranger turned aside into a thick fir-wood, and disappeared, rattling amongst the tangled branches.

Slowly and thoughtfully, Sintram rode on towards his father's castle, his horse now again quiet and altogether exhausted. He scarcely knew how much he ought to relate of his wonderful journey. He also felt oppressed with anxiety for the good Rolf, who had remained so far behind.

He found himself at the castle-gate sooner than he had expected. The drawbridge was lowered, the doors were thrown open. An attendant led Sintram into the Great Hall, where Biorn was sitting all alone at a huge table, with many flagons and glasses before him, and suits of armour ranged on either side of him. As part of his daily custom, and by way of company, Biorn had the armour of his ancestors, with closed visors, placed round the table at which he sat. Father and son began conversing as follows:

"Where is Rolf?"

"I do not know, father. He left me in the mountains."

"I will have Rolf shot if he cannot take better care than that of my only child."

"Then, father, you will have your only child shot at the same time, for without Rolf I cannot live. And if even one single dart is aimed at him, I will be there to receive it, and to shield his true and faithful heart."

"Is that so? Then Rolf shall not be shot, but he shall

be driven from the castle."

"In that case, father, you will see me go away also, and I will give myself up to serve him in forests, in mountains, in caves."

"Is that so? Well, then, Rolf must remain here."

"That is just what I think, father."

"Were you riding quite alone?"

"No, father, but with a strange pilgrim who said that he knew you very well, perhaps too well." Then Sintram began to relate and to describe all that had passed with the pale man.

"I also know him very well," said Biorn. "He is half crazed and half wise, as we sometimes are astonished at seeing that people can be. But do go rest, my boy, after your wild journey. I give you my word that Rolf shall be kindly received if he arrives here, and that if he does not come soon, he shall be sought for in the mountains."

"I trust your word, father," said Sintram, half-humble, half-proud; and he did as commanded by the grim Lord of the Castle.

CHAPTER IV

The Pilgrim and the Knight

TOWARDS evening Sintram awoke. He saw the good Rolf sitting at his bedside, and looked up in the old man's kind face with a smile of unusually innocent brightness. Soon, however, his dark brows were knit again, and he asked, "How did my father receive you, Rolf? Did he say a harsh word to you?"

"No, my dear young lord, he did not. Indeed, he did not speak to me at all. At first, he looked very wrathful, but he checked himself, and ordered a servant to bring me food and wine to refresh me, and afterwards to take me to your room."

"He might have kept his word better, but he is my father, and I must not judge him too harshly. I will now go down to the evening meal." So saying, he sprang up and threw on his furred mantle.

But Rolf stopped him, and said, entreatingly, "My dear young master, you would do better to take your meal today alone, here in your own apartment, for there is a guest with your father, in whose company I should be very sorry to see you. If you will remain here, I will entertain you with pleasant tales and songs."

"There is nothing in the world which I should like better, dear Rolf," answered Sintram, "but it would not be appropriate for me to shun any man. Tell me, whom should I find with my father?"

"Alas!" said the old man, "you have already found him in the mountain. Formerly, when I used to ride about the country with Biorn, we often met with him, but I was forbidden to tell you anything about him. This is the first time that he has ever come to the castle."

"The Crazy Pilgrim!" replied Sintram, and he stood awhile in deep thought, as if considering the matter. At last, rousing himself, he said, "Dear old friend, I would most willingly stay here this evening, all alone with you and your stories and songs, and all the pilgrims in the world should not entice me from this quiet room.

"But one thing must be considered. I feel a kind of dread of that tall pale man, and by such fears no knight's son can ever allow himself to be overcome. So, be not angry, dear Rolf, if I determine to go and look that strange pilgrim in the face." And he shut the door of the chamber behind him and, with firm and echoing steps, proceeded to the hall.

The pilgrim and the knight were sitting opposite each other at the great table, on which many lights were burning; and it was fearful, amongst all the lifeless armour, to see those two tall grim men move, and eat, and drink.

As the pilgrim looked up on the boy's entrance, Biorn

said, "You know him already. He is my only child and your fellow traveller this morning."

The pilgrim fixed an earnest look on Sintram, and answered, shaking his head, "I know not what you mean."

Then the boy burst forth, impatiently, "It must be confessed that you deal very unfairly with us! You say that you know my father too well, and now it seems that you know me altogether too little. Look me in the face. Who allowed you to ride on his horse and, in return, had his good steed driven almost wild? Speak, if you can!"

Biorn smiled, shaking his head, but well pleased, as was his customary attitude with his son's wild behaviour. Meanwhile, the pilgrim shuddered, as if terrified and overcome by some fearful irresistible power.

At length, with a trembling voice, he said these words, "Yes, yes, my dear young lord, you are surely quite right. You are perfectly right in everything that you may please to assert."

Then the Lord of the Castle laughed aloud, and said, "Why, you strange pilgrim, what is become of all your wonderfully fine speeches and warnings now? Has the boy all at once struck you dumb and powerless? Beware, you prophet-messenger, beware!"

However, the pilgrim cast a fearful look on Biorn, which seemed to quench the light of his fiery eyes, and said solemnly, in a thundering voice, "Between me and you, old man, the case stands quite otherwise. We have nothing to reproach each other with. And now suffer me to sing a song to you on the lute."

He stretched out his hand, and took down from the

wall a forgotten and half-strung lute, which was hanging there; and, having put it in a state fit for use, he struck some chords with surprising skill and briskness, and raised this song to the low melancholy tones of the instrument:

> *The flow'ret was mine own, mine own,*
> *But I have lost its fragrance rare,*
> *And knightly name and freedom fair,*
> *Through sin, through sin alone.*
>
> *The flow'ret was thine own, thine own,*
> *Why cast away what thou didst win?*
> *Thou knight no more, but slave of sin,*
> *Thou'rt fearfully alone!*

"Have a care!" shouted he at the close in a pealing voice, as he pulled the strings so mightily that they all broke with a clanging wail, and a cloud of dust rose from the old lute, which spread round him like a mist.

Sintram had been watching him narrowly whilst he was singing, and more and more did he feel convinced that it was impossible that this man and his fellow traveller of the morning could be one and the same. The doubt rose to certainty, when the stranger again looked round at him with the same timid anxious air and, with many excuses and low reverences, hung the lute in its old place, and then ran out of the hall as if bewildered with terror, in strange contrast with the proud and stately bearing that he had shown to Biorn.

The eyes of the boy were now directed to his father, and he saw that Biorn had sunk back senseless in his seat, as if struck by a blow. Sintram's cries called Rolf and other attendants into the hall, and only by great labour did their united efforts awake the Lord of the Castle. His looks were still wild and disordered, but he allowed himself to be taken to rest, quiet and yielding.

CHAPTER V

A Surprise Assault from the Shore

AN illness followed this sudden attack; and, during the course of it, the stout old knight, in the midst of his delirious ravings, did not cease to affirm confidently that he must and should recover. He laughed proudly when his fits of fever came on, and rebuked them for daring to attack him so needlessly. Then he murmured to himself, "That was not the right one yet. There must still be another one out in the cold mountains."

Always at such words, Sintram involuntarily shuddered. They seemed to strengthen his notion that he who had ridden with him, and he who had sat at table in the castle, were two quite distinct persons; and he did not know why, but this thought was inexpressibly awful to him.

Biorn recovered, and appeared to have entirely forgotten his adventure with the pilgrim. He hunted in the mountains; he carried on his usual wild warfare with his neighbours; and Sintram, as he grew up, became his almost constant companion. And, each year, a fearful strength of body and spirit was unfolded in the youth.

Everyone trembled at the sight of Sintram's sharp pallid features, his dark rolling eyes, his tall and muscular and somewhat lean form; and yet no one hated him – not even those whom he distressed or injured in his wildest humours.

This arose, in part, out of regard to old Rolf, who seldom left him for long, and who always held a softening influence over him; but also many of those who had known the Lady Verena, while she still lived in the world, agreed that a faint reflection of her heavenly expression floated over the very unlike features of her son, and that, by this, their hearts were won.

Once, just at the beginning of Spring, Biorn and his son were hunting in the neighbourhood of the seacoast, over a tract of country which did not belong to them; drawn there less by the love of sport, more by the wish of demonstrating defiance to a chieftain whom they detested, and thus provoking a feud.

At that season of the year, when his winter dreams had just passed off, Sintram was always unusually fierce and disposed toward warlike adventures. And this day he was enraged at the chieftain for not coming in arms from his castle to hinder their hunting; and he cursed, in the wildest words, the man's tame patience and love of peace.

Just then, one of his wild young companions rushed towards him, shouting joyfully, "Be content, my dear young lord! I will wager that all is coming about as we and you wish, for as I was pursuing a wounded deer down to the seashore, I saw a sail and a vessel filled with armed men making for the shore. Doubtless, your enemy intends to attack you from the coast."

Joyfully and secretly, Sintram called all his followers together, being resolved this time to take the combat on himself, alone, and then to rejoin his father, and astonish him with the sight of captured foes and other tokens of victory.

The hunters, thoroughly acquainted with every cliff and rock on the coast, hid themselves round the landing place, and soon the strange vessel heaved nearer with swelling sails, until it came to anchor, and its crew began to disembark in unsuspecting security.

At the head of them appeared a knight of high degree, in blue steel armour, richly inlaid with gold. His head was bare, for he carried his costly golden helmet hanging on his left arm. He looked royally around him; and his countenance, which dark brown locks shaded, was pleasant to behold; and a well-trimmed moustache fringed his mouth, from which, as he smiled, gleamed forth two rows of pearly white teeth.

A feeling came across Sintram that he must already have seen this knight somewhere; and he stood motionless for a few moments. But suddenly he raised his hand, to make the agreed signal of attack.

In vain did the good Rolf, who had just succeeded in getting up to him, whisper in his ear that these could not be the foes whom he had taken them for, but that they were unknown, and certainly high and noble strangers.

"Let them be who they may," replied the wild youth, "they have enticed me here to wait, and they shall pay the penalty of fooling me. Say not another word, if you value your life." And immediately, when he gave the signal, a thick shower of javelins followed from all sides, and the Norwegian warriors rushed forth with flashing swords.

They found their foes as brave, or somewhat braver, than they could have desired. More fell on the side of those who made the assault than of those who received it; and the strangers appeared to understand, surprisingly, the Norwegian manner of fighting.

In his haste, the knight in steel armour had not put on his helmet. However, it seemed as if he had no need of such protection, for his good sword afforded him sufficient defence, even against the spears and darts that were incessantly hurled at him, as, with rapid skill, he received them on the shining blade and dashed them far away, shattered into fragments.

During the first assault, Sintram could not penetrate to where this shining hero was standing, as all his followers, eager after such a noble prey, thronged closely round him; but now the way cleared enough for him to spring towards the brave stranger, shouting a war cry, and brandishing his sword above his head.

"Gabrielle!" cried the knight, as he dexterously parried the heavy blow which was descending, and with one powerful sword-thrust he laid the youth prostrate on the ground; then placing his knee on Sintram's breast, he drew forth a flashing dagger, and held it before Sintram's eyes as he lay astonished.

All at once, the men-at-arms stood round like walls. Sintram felt that no hope remained for him. Determined to die as would become a bold warrior, he looked on the fatal weapon with a steady gaze and with not one sign of emotion.

As he lay with his eyes cast upwards, Sintram fancied that there appeared suddenly, from Heaven, a wondrously beautiful female form in bright attire of blue and gold. "Our ancestors told truly of the Valkyries," he murmured. "Strike, then, you unknown conqueror." However, the knight did not comply.

Neither was it a Valkyrie who had so suddenly appeared. Indeed, it was the beautiful wife of the stranger, who, having advanced to the high edge of the vessel, met the upraised look of Sintram. "Folko," cried she, in the softest tone, "you knight without reproach! I know that you spare the vanquished."

The knight sprang up and, with courtly grace, stretched out his hand to the conquered youth, saying, "Thank the noble Lady of Montfaucon for your life and liberty. Nevertheless, if you are so totally devoid of all goodness as to wish to resume the combat, here am I. Let it be yours to begin."

Sintram sank, deeply ashamed, on his knees, and wept, for he had often heard speak of the high renown of the French Knight, Folko of Montfaucon, who was related to his father's house, and of the grace and beauty of his gentle lady, Gabrielle.

CHAPTER VI

The Knight and His Lady

THE Lord of Montfaucon looked with astonishment at his strange foe and, as he gazed on him more and more, recollections arose in his mind of that northern race from whom he was descended, and with whom he had always maintained friendly relations. A golden bear's claw, with which Sintram's cloak was fastened, at length made all clear to him.

"Have you not," said he, "a valiant and far-famed kinsman, called the Sea-King Arinbiorn, who carries on his helmet golden vulture wings? And is not your father the Knight Biorn? For surely the bear's claw on your mantle must be the cognisance[2] of your house."

Sintram assented to all this, in deep and humble shame.

The Knight of Montfaucon raised him from the ground, and said gravely, yet gently, "We are, then, of kin, but I could never have believed that anyone of our noble house would attack a peaceful man without provocation, and that, too, without giving warning."

"Slay me at once," answered Sintram, "if indeed I am worthy to die by so noble hands. I can no longer endure the light of day."

"Because you have been overcome?" asked Montfaucon.

Sintram shook his head.

"Or is it, rather, because you have committed an unknightly action?"

The glow of shame that overspread the youth's countenance said, 'Yes' to this.

"But you should not, on that account, wish to die," continued Montfaucon. "You should rather wish to live, that you may prove your repentance, and make your name illustrious by many noble deeds. For you are endowed with a bold spirit and strength of limb, also with the eagle glance of a chieftain. I should have made you a knight this very hour, if you had borne yourself as bravely in a good cause as you have just now in a bad. See to it, that I may do it soon. You may yet become a vessel of high honour."

A joyous sound of shawms[3] and rebecks[4] interrupted his discourse.

The Lady Gabrielle, bright as the morning, had now come down from the ship, surrounded by her maidens. Appraised by Folko, she took the combat as some mere trial of arms, saying, "You must not be cast down, noble youth, because my wedded lord has won the prize, for be it known to you, that in the whole world there is but one knight who can boast of not having been overcome by the Baron of Montfaucon.

"And who can say," she continued, sportingly, "whether even that would have happened, had he not set himself to win back the magic ring from me, his lady-love, destined to him by the choice of my own heart as well as by the will of Heaven!"

Folko, smiling, bent his head over the snow-white hand of his lady, and then bade the youth conduct them to his father's castle.

Rolf took upon himself to see to the disembarking of the horses and valuables of the strangers, filled with joy at the thought that an angel in woman's form had appeared to soften his beloved young master, and perhaps even to free him from that early curse.

Sintram sent messengers in all directions to seek for his father, and to announce to him the arrival of his noble guests. They therefore found the old knight in his castle, with everything prepared for their reception.

Gabrielle could not enter the vast dark-looking building without a slight shudder, which was increased when she saw the rolling fiery eyes of its lord. Even the pale dark-haired Sintram seemed to her very fearful, and she sighed to herself, "Oh! What an awful abode have you brought me to visit, my knight! How I wish that we were once again in my sunny Gascony or in your knightly Normandy!"

But the grave yet courteous reception, the deep respect paid to her grace and beauty, and to the high fame of Folko, helped to reassure her; and soon her bird-like pleasure in novelties was awakened through the strange significant appearance of this new world. And besides, it could only be for a passing moment that any womanly fears found a place in her breast when her lord was near at hand, for she knew well what effectual protection that brave Baron was ever ready to render to all those who were dear to him, or committed to his charge.

Soon afterwards, Rolf passed through the Great Hall, in which Biorn and his guests were seated, conducting their attendants, who had charge of the baggage, to their rooms.

Gabrielle caught sight of her favourite lute, and desired a page to bring it to her, that she might see if the precious instrument had been injured by the sea voyage. As she bent over it with earnest attention, and her taper fingers ran up and down the strings, a smile, like the dawn of spring, passed over the dark countenances of Biorn and his son; and both said, with an involuntary sigh, "Ah! If you would but play on that lute, and sing to it! It would be but too beautiful!"

The lady looked up at them, well pleased, and smiling her assent, she began this song:

> *Songs and flowers are returning*
> *And radiant skies of May,*
> *Earth her choicest gifts is yielding,*
> *But one is past away.*
>
> *The spring that clothes with tend'rest green*
> *Each grove and sunny plain,*
> *Shines not for my forsaken heart,*
> *Brings not my joys again.*

Warble not so, thou nightingale,
Upon thy blooming spray,
Thy sweetness now will burst my heart,
I cannot bear thy lay.

For flowers and birds are come again,
And breezes mild of May,
But treasured hopes and golden hours
Are lost to me for aye!

The two Norwegians sat plunged in melancholy thought; but especially Sintram's eyes began to brighten with a milder expression, his cheeks glowed, every feature softened, until those who looked at him could have fancied they saw a glorified spirit.

At that point, the good Rolf, who had stood listening to the song, rejoiced from his heart, and devoutly raised his hands in pious gratitude to Heaven.

But Gabrielle's astonishment would not allow her to take her eyes from Sintram. At last, she said to him, "I should much like to know what has so struck you in that little song. It is merely a simple lay of spring, full of the images which that sweet season never fails to call up in the minds of my countrymen."

"But is your home really so lovely, so wondrously rich in song?" cried the enraptured Sintram. "Then I am no longer surprised at your heavenly beauty, at the power which you exercise over my hard wayward heart! For a paradise of song must surely send such angelic messengers through the ruder parts of the world." And so saying, he fell on his knees before the lady, in an attitude of deep humility.

All the while, Folko looked on with an approving smile, whilst Gabrielle, in much embarrassment, seemed hardly to know how to treat the half-wild half-tamed young stranger. After some hesitation, however, she held out her fair hand to him, and said, as she gently raised him, "Surely one who listens with such delight to music must himself know how to awaken its strains. Take my lute, and let us hear a graceful inspired song."

But Sintram drew back, and would not take the instrument. He said, "Heaven forbid that my rough untutored hand should touch those delicate strings! For even were I to begin with some soft strains, before long the wild spirit which dwells in me would break out, and there would be an end to the form and sound of the beautiful instrument. No, no, allow me instead to fetch my own huge harp, strung with bears' sinews set in brass, for in truth I do feel myself inspired to play and sing."

Gabrielle murmured a half-frightened assent; and Sintram, having quickly brought his harp, began to strike it loudly, and to sing these words, with a voice no less powerful:

> 'Sir Knight, Sir Knight, oh! Whither away
>   'With thy snow-white sail on the foaming spray?'
>   Sing heigh, sing ho, for that land of flowers!

> 'Too long have I trod upon ice and snow;
>   I seek the bowers where roses blow.'
>   Sing heigh, sing ho, for that land of flowers!

He steer'd on his course by night and day
Till he cast his anchor in Naples Bay.
Sing heigh, sing ho, for that land of flowers!

There wander'd a lady upon the strand,
Her fair hair bound with a golden band.
Sing heigh, sing ho, for that land of flowers!

'Hail to thee! Hail to thee! Lady Bright,
Mine own shalt thou be ere morning light.'
Sing heigh, sing ho, for that land of flowers!

'Not so, Sir Knight," the lady replied,
'For you speak to the margrave's chosen bride.'
Sing heigh, sing ho, for that land of flowers!

'Your lover may come with his shield and spear,
And the victor shall win thee, lady dear!'
Sing heigh, sing ho, for that land of flowers!

'Nay, seek for another bride, I pray;
Most fair are the maidens of Naples Bay.'
Sing heigh, sing ho, for that land of flowers!

'No, lady; for thee my heart doth burn,
And the world cannot now my purpose turn.'
Sing heigh, sing ho, for that land of flowers!

Then came the young margrave, bold and brave;
But low was he laid in a grassy grave.
Sing heigh, sing ho, for that land of flowers!

> *And then the fierce Northman joyously cried,*
> *'Now shall I possess lands, castle, and bride!'*
> *Sing heigh, sing ho, for that land of flowers!*

Sintram's song was ended, but his eyes glared wildly, and the vibrations of the harp strings still resounded in a marvellous manner.

Biorn's attitude was again erect; he stroked his long beard and rattled his sword, as if in great delight at what he had just heard.

Gabrielle shuddered much before the wild song and these strange forms, but only until she cast a glance on the Lord of Montfaucon, sat there smiling in all his hero strength, unmoved, while the rough uproar passed by him like an autumnal storm.

CHAPTER VII

A Tale of Ancient Greece

SOME weeks after this, in the twilight of evening, Sintram, very disturbed, came down to the castle garden. Although the presence of Gabrielle never failed to soothe and calm him, if she left the apartment for even a few instants, the fearful wildness of his spirit seemed to return with renewed strength.

So even now, after having long and kindly read legends of the olden times to his father Biorn, she had retired to her chamber. The tones of her lute could be distinctly heard in the garden below, but the sounds only drove the bewildered youth more impetuously through the shades of the ancient elms.

Stooping suddenly to avoid some overhanging branches, he unexpectedly came upon something against which he had almost struck, and which, at first sight, he took for a small bear standing on its hind legs, with a long and strangely crooked horn on its head.

He drew back in surprise and fear. It addressed him in a grating man's voice, "Well, my brave young knight, from what place do you come? To what place do you go? For what reason are you so terrified?"

And then, for the first time, Sintram saw that he had before him a little old man, so wrapped up in a rough garment of fur that scarcely one of his features was visible, and wearing, in his cap, a strange looking long feather.

"But from what place do *you* come and to what place do *you* go?" returned the angry Sintram. "Of you, such questions should be asked. What have you to do in our realms, you hideous little being?"

"Well, well," sneered the other one, "I am thinking that I am quite big enough as I am — one cannot always be a giant. And as to the rest, why should you find fault that I go here hunting for snails? Surely, snails do not belong to the game that your high mightinesses consider that you alone have a right to follow!

"Now, on the other hand, I know how to prepare from them an excellent high-flavoured drink, and I have taken enough today. Marvellous fat little beasts, with wise faces like a man's, and long twisted horns on their heads. Would you like to see them? Look here!" And then he began to unfasten and fumble about his fur garment.

But Sintram, filled with disgust and horror, said, "I detest such animals! Be quiet, and tell me at once who and what you yourself are."

"Are you so bent upon knowing my name?" replied the little man. "Let it content you that I am Master of all secret knowledge, and well versed in the most intricate depths of ancient history. Ah, my young sir, if you would only hear them! But you are afraid of me."

"Afraid of you!" cried Sintram, with a wild laugh.

"Many a better man than you has been so before now," muttered the Little Master, "but they did not like being told of it anymore than you do."

"To prove that you are mistaken," said Sintram, "I will remain here with you 'til the moon stands high in the heavens. But you must tell me one of your stories in the meantime."

The little man, much pleased, nodded his head; and, as they paced together up and down a retired elm-walk, he began, "Many hundred years ago a young knight, called Paris of Troy, lived in that sunny land of the south where are found the sweetest songs, the brightest flowers, and the most beautiful ladies. You know a song that tells of that fair land, do you not, young sir? 'Sing heigh, sing ho, for that land of flowers.'"

Sintram bowed his head in assent, and sighed deeply.

"Now," resumed the Little Master, "it happened that Paris led that kind of life which is not uncommon in those countries, and of which their poets often sing. He would pass whole months in the garb of a peasant, piping in the woods and mountains and pasturing his flocks.

"Here, one day, three beautiful goddesses appeared to him, disputing about a golden apple. From him they sought to know which of them was the most beautiful, since to her the golden fruit was to be awarded. The first knew how to give thrones, and sceptres, and crowns; the second could give wisdom and knowledge; and the third could prepare love-potions and love-charms, which could not fail in securing the affections of the fairest of women.

"Each one, in turn, proffered her choicest gifts to the young shepherd, in order that, tempted by them, he might adjudge the apple to her. But as fair women charmed him more than anything else did in the world, he said that the third was the most beautiful – her name was Aphrodite.

"The two others, Hera and Athena, departed in great displeasure, but Aphrodite bid him put on his knightly armour and his helmet, adorned with waving feathers, and then she led him to a famous city called Sparta, where ruled the noble King Menelaus. His young Queen, Helen, was the loveliest woman on earth, and the goddess offered her to Paris in return for the golden apple. He was most ready to have her and wished for nothing better, but he asked how he was to gain possession of her."

"Paris must have been a sorry Knight," interrupted Sintram. "Such things are easily settled. The husband is challenged to a single combat, and he that is victorious carries off the wife."

"But King Menelaus was the host of the young knight," said the narrator.

"Listen to me, Little Master," cried Sintram. "He might have asked the goddess for some other beautiful woman, and then have mounted his horse, or weighed anchor, and departed."

"Yes, yes. It is very easy to say so," replied the old man. "But if you only knew how bewitchingly lovely was Queen Helen. There was no room left for a substitute." And then he began a glowing description of the charms of this wondrously beautiful woman, likening the image to Gabrielle so closely, feature for feature, that Sintram, tottering, was forced to lean against a tree.

The Little Master stood opposite to him grinning, and asked, "Well now, could you have advised the poor knight Paris to fly from her?

"Tell me at once what happened next," stammered Sintram.

"The goddess acted honourably towards Paris," continued the old man. "She declared to him that if he would carry away the lovely queen to his own city of Troy, he might do so, and therefore cause the ruin of his whole house and of his country, but during ten years he would be able to defend himself in Troy, and rejoice in the sweet love of Helen."

"And he accepted those terms, or he was a fool!" cried the youth.

"To be sure, he accepted them," whispered the Little Master. "I would have done so in his place! And do you know, young sir, the look of things then was just as they are happening today? The newly risen moon, partly veiled by clouds, was shining dimly through the thick branches of the trees in the silence of evening.

"Leaning against an old tree, as you are doing now, stood the young enamoured knight Paris, and at his side the goddess Aphrodite, but so disguised and transformed, that she did not look much more beautiful than I do. And by the silvery light of the moon, the form of the beautiful beloved one was seen sweeping by, alone amidst the whispering boughs."

He was silent, and as in the mirror of his deluding words, Gabrielle just then actually appeared, musing as she walked alone down the alley of elms.

"Man – fearful Master – by what name shall I call you? To what would you drive me?" muttered the trembling Sintram.

"You know your father's strong stone castle on the Rocks of the Moon?" replied the old man. "The castellan and the garrison are true and devoted to you. It could stand a ten years' siege, and the little gate, which leads to the hills, is open, as was that of the citadel of Sparta for Paris."

And, in fact, the youth saw through a gate – left open he knew not how – the dim distant mountains glittering in the moonlight. "And if he did not accept, he was a fool," said the Little Master, with a grin, echoing Sintram's former words.

At that moment, Gabrielle stood close by him. She was within reach of his grasp, had he made the least movement. A moonbeam, suddenly breaking forth, transfigured, as it were, her heavenly beauty.

The youth had already bent forward –

> *My Lord and God, I pray,*
> *Turn from his heart away*
> *This world's turmoil;*
>
> *And call him to Thy light,*
> *Be it through sorrow's night,*
> *Through pain or toil.*

These words were sung by old Rolf at that very time, as he lingered on the still margin of the castle fishpond, where he prayed alone to Heaven, full of foreboding care.

They reached Sintram's ear. He stood, as if spellbound, and made the Sign of the Cross.

Immediately, the Little Master fled away, jumping uncouthly on one leg, through the gates and shutting them after him with a yell.

Gabrielle shuddered, terrified at the wild noise.

Sintram approached her softly, and said, offering his arm to her, "Allow me to lead you back to the castle. The night in these northern regions is often wild and fearful."

CHAPTER VIII

The Merchants of Hamburg

THEY found, within, the two knights drinking wine. Folko was relating stories, in his usual mild and cheerful manner, and Biorn was listening with a moody air, yet as if – against his will – the dark cloud might pass away before that bright and gentle courtesy.

Gabrielle saluted the Baron with a smile, and signed to him to continue his discourse, as she took her place near the knight Biorn, full of watchful kindness.

Sintram stood by the hearth, abstracted and melancholy; and the embers, as he stirred them, cast a strange glow over his pallid features.

"And of all the German trading towns," continued Montfaucon, "the largest and richest is Hamburg. In Normandy, we willingly see their merchants land on our coasts, and those excellent people never fail to prove themselves our friends when we seek their advice and assistance. When I first visited Hamburg, every honour and respect was paid to me. I found its inhabitants engaged in a war with a neighbouring Count, and immediately I used my sword for them, vigorously and successfully."

"Your sword! Your knightly sword!" interrupted Biorn, and the old customary fire flashed from his eyes. "Against a knight! And for shopkeepers!"

"Sir Knight," replied Folko, calmly, "the Barons of Montfaucon have ever used their swords as they chose, without the interference of another. And, as I have received this good custom, so do I wish to hand it on. If you agree not to this, so speak it freely out. But I forbid every rude word against the men of Hamburg, since I have declared them to be my friends."

Biorn cast down his haughty eyes, and their fire faded away. In a low voice he said, "Proceed, noble Baron. You are right, and I am wrong."

Then Folko stretched out his hand to him across the table, and resumed his narration, "Amongst all my beloved Hamburgers, the dearest to me are two men of marvellous experience – a father and son. What have they not seen and done in the remotest corners of the earth, and instituted in their native town! Praise be to God, my life cannot be called unfruitful, but, compared with the wise Gotthard Lenz and his stout-hearted son Rudlieb, I look upon myself as an esquire who has perhaps been to a few times tourneys[5], and, besides that, has never hunted out his own forests.

"They have converted, subdued, gladdened dark men whom I know not how to name, and the wealth which they have brought back with them has all been devoted to the common state of wealth, as if fit for no other purpose.

"On their return from their long and perilous sea voyages, they hasten to a hospital, which has been founded by them, and where they undertake the part of overseers, and of careful and patient nurses. Then they proceed to select the most fitting spots to erect new towers and fortresses for the defence of their beloved country. Next, they repair to the houses where strangers and travellers receive hospitality at their cost. And, at last, they return to their own abode, to entertain their guests, rich and noble like kings, and simple and unconstrained like shepherds.

"Many a tale of their wondrous adventures serves to enliven these sumptuous feasts. Amongst others, I remember to have heard my friends relate one at which my hair stood on end. Possibly, I may gain some more complete information on the subject from you.

"It appears that several years ago, just about the time of the Christmas festival, Gotthard and Rudlieb were shipwrecked on the coast of Norway, during a violent winter tempest. They could never exactly ascertain the situation of the rocks on which their vessel stranded. But, so much is certain, that very near the seashore stood a huge castle, to which the father and son applied themselves, seeking that assistance and shelter which Christian people are ever willing to afford each other in case of need.

"They went alone, leaving their followers to watch the injured ship. The castle-gates were thrown open, and they thought all was well. But, all of a sudden, the courtyard was filled with armed men, who, with one accord, aimed their sharp iron-pointed spears at the defenceless strangers, whose dignified remonstrances and mild entreaties were only heard in sullen silence or with scornful jeerings.

"After a while, a knight came down the stairs, with fire-flashing eyes. They hardly knew whether to think they saw a spectre, or a wild heathen. He gave a signal, and the fatal spears closed around them. At that instant, the soft tones of a woman's voice fell on their ear, calling on the Saviour's holy name for aid. At the sound, the spectres in the courtyard rushed madly one against the other, the gates burst open, and Gotthard and Rudlieb fled away, catching a glimpse as they went of an angelic woman who appeared at one of the windows of the castle.

"They made every exertion to get their ship again afloat, choosing to trust themselves to the sea rather than to that barbarous coast, and at last, after manifold dangers, they landed at Denmark. They say that some heathen must have owned the cruel castle, but I hold it to be some ruined fortress, deserted by men, in which hellish spectres were in the habit of holding their nightly meetings. What heathen could be found so demon-like as to offer death to shipwrecked strangers, instead of refreshment and shelter?"

Biorn gazed fixedly on the ground, as though he were turned into stone, but Sintram came towards the table, and said, "Father, let us seek out this godless abode, and lay it level with the dust. I cannot tell how, but somehow I feel quite sure that the accursed deed of which we have just heard is the cause of my frightful dreams."

Enraged at his son, Biorn rose, and would perhaps again have uttered some dreadful words, but Heaven decreed otherwise, for at that moment the pealing notes of a trumpet were heard, which drowned out the angry tones of his voice.

The great doors opened slowly, and a herald entered the hall. He bowed reverently, and then said, "I am sent by Jarl Eric the Aged. He returned two days ago from his expedition to the Grecian seas. His wish had been to take vengeance on the island, which is called Chios, where fifty years ago his father was slain by the soldiers of the Emperor. But your kinsman, the Sea-King Arinbiorn, who was lying there at anchor, tried to pacify him.

"To this, Jarl Eric would not listen, so the Sea-King said next that he would never suffer Chios to be laid waste, because it was an island where the lays of an old Greek bard, called Homer, were excellently sung, and where, moreover, a very choice wine was made.

"Words proving of no avail, a combat ensued, in which Arinbiorn had so much the advantage that Jarl Eric lost two of his ships, and only with difficulty escaped in one which had already sustained great damage. Eric the Aged has now resolved to take revenge on some of the Sea-King's race, since Arinbiorn himself is seldom on the spot.

"Will you, Biorn of the Fiery Eyes, at once pay – in cattle, and money, and goods – the penalty in full, as it may please the Jarl to demand? Or will you prepare to meet him with an armed force at Niflung's Heath seven days from now?"

Biorn bowed his head quietly, and replied in a mild tone, "Seven days hence at Niflung's Heath." To the herald, he then offered a golden goblet full of rich wine, and added, "Drink that, and then carry off with you the cup that you have emptied."

"The Baron of Montfaucon likewise sends greeting to your chieftain, Jarl Eric," interposed Folko, "and also engages to be at Niflung's Heath, as the hereditary friend of the Sea-King as well as the kinsman and guest of Biorn of the Fiery Eyes."

The herald was seen to tremble at the name of Montfaucon. He bowed very low, cast an anxious reverential look at the Baron, and left the hall.

Gabrielle looked on her Knight, smiling lovingly and securely, for she well knew his victorious prowess, and she only asked, "Where shall I remain, while you go forth to battle, Folko?"

"I had hoped," answered Biorn, "that you would be well contented to stay in this castle, lovely lady. I leave my son to guard you and attend on you."

Gabrielle hesitated an instant, and Sintram, who had resumed his position near the fire, muttered to himself, as he fixed his eyes on the bright flames that were flashing up, "Yes, yes, so it will probably happen. I can fancy that King Menelaus had just left Sparta on some warlike expedition, when the young knight Paris met the lovely Helen that evening in the garden."

But Gabrielle, shuddering, although she knew not why, said quickly, "Without you, Folko? And must I forego the joy of seeing you fight? Or the honour of tending you, should you chance to receive a wound?"

Folko bowed, gracefully thanking his lady, and

replied, "Come with your knight, since it is your pleasure, and be to him a bright guiding star. It is a good old northern custom that ladies should be present at knightly combats, and no true warrior of the north will fail to respect the place where beams the light of their eyes. Unless, indeed," continued he, with an inquiring look at Biorn, "unless Jarl Eric is not worthy of his forefather?"

"A man of honour," said Biorn confidently.

"Then array yourself, my fairest love," said the delighted Folko. "Array yourself and come with us to the battlefield to behold and judge our deeds."

"Come with us to the battle," echoed Sintram in a sudden transport of joy.

And they all dispersed in calm cheerfulness; Sintram taking himself again to the wood, while the others retired to rest.

CHAPTER IX

The Battle on Niflung's Heath

THE tract of country that bore the name of Niflung's Heath was wild and dreary. According to tradition, the young Niflung, son of Hogni, the last of his race, had darkly ended there a sad and unsuccessful life.

Many ancient gravestones were still standing round about, and in the few oak trees scattered here and there over the plain, huge eagles had built their nests. The beating of their heavy wings as they fought together, and their wild screams, was heard far off in more thickly peopled regions. And, at the sound, children would tremble in their cradles, and old men quake with fear as they slumbered over the blazing hearth.

As the seventh night, the last before the day of combat, was just beginning, two large armies were seen descending from the hills in opposite directions. That which came from the west was commanded by Eric the Aged, and that which came from the east by Biorn of the Fiery Eyes.

They appeared early in compliance with the custom

that required adversaries should always present themselves at the appointed field of battle before the time named, in order to prove that they sought, rather than dreaded, the fight.

On the most convenient spot, Folko immediately pitched his tent of blue samite[6] fringed with gold, which he carried with him to shelter his gentle lady. Meanwhile, Sintram, in the role of herald, rode over to Jarl Eric to announce to him that the beauteous Gabrielle of Montfaucon was present in the army of the Knight Biorn, and, the next morning, would be present as a judge of the combat.

Jarl Eric bowed low on receiving this pleasing message; and ordered his bards to strike up a lay:

> *Warriors bold of Eric's band,*
> *Gird your glittering armour on,*
> *Stand beneath to-morrow's sun,*
> > *In your might.*

> *Fairest dame that ever gladden'd*
> *Our wild shores with beauty's vision,*
> *May thy bright eyes o'er our combat,*
> > *Judge the right!*

> *Tidings of yon noble stranger*
> *Long ago have reach'd our ears,*
> *Wafted upon southern breezes,*
> > *O'er the wave.*

Now midst yonder hostile ranks,
In his warlike pride he meets us,
Folko comes! Fight, men of Eric,
       True and brave!

These wondrous tones floated over the plain, and reached the tent of Gabrielle. It was no new thing to her to hear her knight's fame celebrated on all sides, but now that she listened to his praises bursting forth in the stillness of night from the mouth of his enemies, she could scarce refrain from kneeling at the feet of the mighty chieftain.

But he, with courteous tenderness, held her up, and pressing his lips fervently on her soft hand, he said, "My deeds, oh lovely lady, belong to you, and not to me!"

Now the night had passed away, and the east was glowing; and on Niflung's Heath, there was waving, and resounding, and glowing too. Knights put on their rattling armour, warhorses began to neigh, and the morning draught went round in gold and silver goblets, while war-songs and the clang of harps resounded in the midst.

A joyous march was heard in Biorn's camp, as Montfaucon, with his troops and retainers, clad in bright steel armour, conducted their lady up to a neighbouring hill, where she would be safe from the spears that would soon be flying in all directions, and from where she could look freely over the battlefield. The morning sun, as if it were in homage, played over her beauty; and as she came in view of the camp of Jarl Eric, his soldiers lowered their weapons, whilst the chieftains bent low the crests of their huge helmets.

Two of Montfaucon's pages remained in attendance on Gabrielle; willingly curbing their love of fighting for so noble a service. Both armies passed in front of her, saluting her and singing as they went; they then placed themselves in array, and the fight began.

The spears flew from the hands of the stout northern warriors, rattling against the broad shields under which they sheltered themselves, or sometimes clattering as they met in the air. At intervals, on one side or the other, a man was struck and fell silent in his blood.

Then the Knight of Montfaucon advanced with his troop of Norman horsemen. Even as he dashed past, he did not fail to lower his shining sword to salute Gabrielle; and then with an exulting war cry, which burst from many a voice, they charged the left wing of the enemy.

Eric's foot soldiers, kneeling firmly, received them with fixed javelins. Many a noble horse fell, wounded to death, and, in falling, brought his rider with him to the ground; others crushed their foes under them in their death-fall. He and his warhorse unwounded, Folko rushed through, followed by a troop of chosen knights.

Already Eric's foot soldiers were falling into disorder, already Biorn's warriors were giving shouts of victory, when a troop of horse, headed by Jarl Eric himself, advanced against the valiant Baron. And while his Normans, hastily assembled, assisted him in repelling this new attack, the enemy's infantry were gradually forming themselves into a thick mass, which rolled on and on.

All these movements seemed caused by a warrior,

whose loud piercing shout was in the midst. And scarcely were the troops formed into this strange array, when suddenly they spread themselves out on all sides, carrying everything before them with the irresistible force of the burning torrent from Hekla[7].

Biorn's soldiers, who had thought to enclose their enemies, lost courage, and gave way before this wondrous onset. In vain, the knight himself attempted to stem the tide of fugitives, and, with difficulty, escaped being carried away by it.

Sintram stood, looking on this scene of confusion with mute indignation. Friends and foes passed by him, all equally avoiding him, and dreading to come in contact with one whose physical appearance was so fearful, almost unearthly, in his motionless rage.

He aimed no blow either to his right or left – his powerful battleaxe at rest in his hand – but his eyes flashed fire, and seemed to be piercing the enemy's ranks through and through, as if he would find out who it was that had conjured up this sudden warlike spirit.

He succeeded. A small man clothed in strange-looking armour, with large golden horns on his helmet, and a long visor advancing in front of it, was leaning on a two-edged curved spear, and seemed to be looking with derision at the flight of Biorn's troops, as they were pursued by their victorious foes.

"That is he," cried Sintram, "he who will drive us from the field before the eyes of Gabrielle!" And, with the swiftness of an arrow, he flew towards the small man with a wild shout.

The combat was fierce, but not of long duration. To the wondrous dexterity of his adversary, Sintram opposed his far superior size, and he dealt so fearful a blow on the horned helmet, that a stream of blood rushed forth. The small man fell, as if stunned, and after some frightful convulsive movements, his limbs appeared to stiffen in death.

His fall gave the signal for of all Eric's army. Even those who had not seen him fall, suddenly lost their courage and eagerness for the battle, and retreated with uncertain steps, or ran in wild terror onto the spears of their enemies.

At the same time, Montfaucon was dispersing Jarl Eric's cavalry. After a desperate conflict, he had hurled their chief from the saddle, and taken him prisoner with his own hand. Biorn of the Fiery Eyes stood victorious in the middle of the field of battle. The day was won.

CHAPTER X

The Unknown Warrior

IN sight of both armies, with glowing cheeks and looks of modest humility, Sintram was conducted by the brave Baron up the hill, where Gabrielle stood in all the lustre of her beauty. Both warriors bent the knee before her, and Folko said, solemnly, "Lady, this valiant youth of a noble race has deserved the reward of this day's victory. I pray you let him receive it from your fair hand."

Gabrielle bowed courteously, took off her scarf of blue and gold, and fastened it to a bright sword, which a page brought to her on a cushion of cloth of silver. Then, with a smile, she presented the noble gift to Sintram, who was bending forward to receive it, when suddenly Gabrielle drew back, and turning to Folko, said, "Noble Baron should not he, on whom I bestow a scarf and sword, be first admitted into the order of knighthood?"

Light as a feather, Folko sprang up, and bowing low before his lady, gave the youth the accolade with solemn earnestness.

Gabrielle then buckled on his sword, saying, "For the

honour of God and the service of virtuous ladies, young knight, I saw you fight, I saw you conquer, and my earnest prayers followed you. Fight and conquer often again, as you have done this day, that the beams of your renown may shine over my far-distant country." And at a sign from Folko, she offered her tender lips for the new knight to kiss.

Thrilling all over, and full of a holy joy, Sintram arose in deep silence, and hot tears streamed down his softened countenance, whilst the shout and the trumpets of the assembled troops greeted the youth with stunning applause.

Old Rolf stood silently on one side, and, as he looked in the mild beaming eyes of his foster-child, he calmly and piously returned thanks:

"The strife at length hath found its end,
Rich blessings now shall Heaven send!
The evil foe is slain!"

All the while, Biorn and Jarl Eric had been talking together eagerly, but not unkindly. The conqueror now led his vanquished enemy up the hill and presented him to the Baron and Gabrielle, saying, "Instead of two enemies you now see two sworn allies. And I request you, my beloved guests and kinsfolk, to receive him graciously as one who, from this time forward, belongs to us."

"He was always so," added Eric, smiling. "I, indeed, sought revenge, but I have now had enough of defeats both by sea and land. Yet I thank Heaven that neither in the Grecian seas, to the Sea-King, nor on Niflung's Heath, to you, have I yielded ingloriously."

The Lord of Montfaucon assented cordially; and, heartily and solemnly, reconciliation was made. Then Jarl Eric addressed Gabrielle with so noble a grace, that with a smile of wonder she gazed on the gigantic grey hero, and gave him her beautiful hand to kiss.

Meanwhile, Sintram was speaking earnestly to his good Rolf, and at length he was heard to say, "But before all, be sure that you bury that wonderfully brave knight whom my battleaxe smote. Choose out the greenest hill for his resting place, and the loftiest oak to shade his grave. Also, I wish you to open his visor and to examine his countenance carefully, that we may not bury him alive, and moreover, that you may be able to describe to me the one to whom I owe the noblest prize of victory."

Rolf bowed readily, and went.

"Our young knight is speaking there of one amongst the slain of whom I should like to hear more," said Folko, turning to Jarl Eric. "Who, dear Jarl, was that wonderful chieftain who led on your troops so skilfully, and who at last fell under Sintram's powerful battleaxe?"

"You ask me more than I know how to answer," replied Jarl Eric. "About three nights ago, this stranger made his appearance amongst us. I was sitting with my chieftains and warriors round the hearth, forging our armour, and singing all the while. Suddenly, above the din of our hammering and our singing, we heard so loud a noise that it silenced us in a moment, and we sat motionless as if we had been turned into stone.

"Before long, the sound was repeated, and at last we made out that it must have been caused by some person blowing a huge horn outside the castle, seeking admittance. I went down to the gate myself, and as I passed through the courtyard, all my dogs were so terrified by the extraordinary noise as to be howling and crouching in their kennels instead of barking.

"I chided them, and called to them, but even the fiercest would not follow me. Then, thought I, I must show you the way to act. So I grasped my sword firmly, I set my torch on the ground close beside me, and I let the gates fly open without further delay, for I knew well that it would be no easy matter for anyone to come in against my will.

"A loud laugh greeted me, and I heard these words, 'Well, well, what mighty preparations are these before one small man can find the shelter he seeks!' And in truth, I did feel myself redden with shame when I saw the small stranger standing opposite to me, quite alone. I called to him to come in at once, and offered my hand to him, but he continued to show some displeasure and would not give me his in return.

"As he went up, however, he became friendlier. He showed me the golden horn on which he sounded that blast, and which he carried screwed onto his helmet, as well as another exactly like it. When he was sitting with us in the hall, he behaved in a very strange manner. Sometimes he was merry, sometimes cross, by turns courteous and rude in his demeanour, without anyone being able to see a motive for such constant changes.

"I longed to know where he came from, but how could I ask my guest such a question? He told us as much as this, that he was starved with cold in our country, and that his own was much warmer. Also, he appeared well acquainted with the city of Constantinople and related fearful stories of how brothers, uncles, nephews, even fathers and sons, thrust each other from the throne, blinded, cut out tongues, and murdered.

"At length, he said his own name – it sounded harmonious, like a Greek name, but none of us could remember it. Before long, he displayed his skill as an armourer. He understood marvellously well how to handle the red-hot iron, and how to form it into more murderous weapons than any I had ever seen before.

"I would not allow him to go on making them, for I was resolved to meet you in the field with equal arms, such as we are all used to in our northern countries. Then he laughed, and said he thought it would be quite possible to be victorious without them, by skilful movements and the like. If only I would entrust the command of my infantry to him, I was sure of victory. Then I thought, he who makes arms well must also wield them well, yet I required some proof of his powers. My lords, he came off victorious in trials of strength such as you can hardly imagine, and although the fame of young Sintram, as a bold and brave warrior, is spread far and wide, I can scarce believe that he could have slain one such as my Greek ally."

Jarl Eric would have continued speaking, but the good Rolf came hastily back with a few followers, the whole party so ghastly pale that all eyes were involuntarily fixed on them, and looked anxiously to hear what tidings they had brought.

Rolf stood still, silent and trembling. "Take courage, my old friend!" cried Sintram. "Whatever you may have to tell is truth and light from your faithful mouth."

"My dear master," began the old man, "do not be angry. But, as to burying that strange warrior whom you slew, it is a thing impossible. Would that we had never opened that wide hideous visor! For so horrible a countenance grinned at us from underneath it, so distorted by death, and with so hellish an expression, that we hardly kept our senses. We could not, by any possibility, have touched him. I would rather be sent to kill wolves and bears in the desert, and look on while fierce birds of prey feast on their carcases."

All present shuddered, and were silent for a time, until Sintram nerved himself to say, "Dear, good old man, why use such wild words as I never heard you utter 'til now? But tell me, Jarl Eric, did your ally appear altogether so awful while he was alive?"

"Not as far as I know," answered Jarl Eric, looking inquiringly at his companions, who were standing around. They said the same thing; but on farther questioning, it appeared that neither the chieftain, nor the knights, nor the soldiers, could say exactly what the stranger looked like.

"We must then find it out for ourselves, and bury the corpse," said Sintram, and he signalled to the assembled party to follow him. All did so, except the Lord of Montfaucon, whom the whispered entreaty of Gabrielle kept at her side. However, Folko lost nothing because of that, for though Niflung's Heath was searched from one end to the other many times, the body of the unknown warrior was no longer to be found.

CHAPTER XI

The Duality of Sintram

THE joyful calm, which came over Sintram on this day, appeared to be more than a passing gleam. If too, at times, a thought of the Knight Paris and Helen would inflame his heart with bolder and wilder wishes, it needed but one look at his scarf and sword and the stream of his inner life glided again clear as a mirror. "What can any man wish for more than has been already bestowed on me?" he would say to himself at such times, serene within. And this went on for a long while.

It chanced one day that Sintram was sitting in the company of Folko and Gabrielle, in almost the very same spot in the garden where he had met that mysterious being whom – without knowing why – he had named the Little Master, but on this day, how different did everything appear! The beautiful northern autumn had already begun to redden the leaves of the oaks and elms round the castle, the sun was sinking slowly over the sea, and the mist of an autumnal evening was rising from the fields and meadows around, towards the hill on which the huge castle stood.

Gabrielle, placing her lute in Sintram's hands, said to him, "Dear friend, as mild and gentle as you now are, I may well dare to entrust to you my tender little darling. Let me again hear you sing that lay of the land of flowers, for I am sure that it will now sound much sweeter than when you accompanied it with the vibrations of your fearful harp."

The young knight bowed as he prepared to obey the lady's commands.

With a grace and softness before now unseen, the tones resounded from his lips, and the wild song appeared to transform itself, and to bloom into a garden of the blessed. Tears stood in Gabrielle's eyes, and Sintram, as he gazed on the pearly brightness, poured forth tones of yet richer sweetness.

When the last notes were sounded, Gabrielle's angelic voice was heard to echo them as she repeated,

Sing heigh, sing ho, for that land of flowers!

Sintram put down the lute, and sighed with a thankful glance towards the stars, now rising in the heavens.

Then Gabrielle, turning towards her lord, murmured these words, "Oh, how long have we been far away from our own shining castles and bright gardens! Oh, to see that land of the sweetest flowers!"

Sintram could scarce believe that he heard correctly, so suddenly did he feel himself shut out from paradise.

But his last hope vanished in the wake of the courteous assurances of Folko that he would endeavour to fulfil his lady's wishes the very next week, and that their ship was lying off the shore ready to put to sea.

Gabrielle thanked him with a kiss imprinted softly on his forehead; and leaning on his arm, she bent her steps, singing and smiling, towards the castle.

Sintram, troubled in mind, as though turned into stone, remained behind, forgotten.

At length, when night was now in the sky, he started up wildly, ran up and down the garden, as if all his former madness had again taken possession of him; and then rushed out and wandered upon the wild moonlit hills. There he dashed his sword against the trees and bushes, so that on all sides was heard a sound of crashing and falling. The birds of night flew about him, screeching in wild alarm; and the deer, startled by the noise, sprang away and took refuge in the thickest thickets.

Abruptly, old Rolf appeared, returning home from a visit to the Chaplain of Drontheim, to whom he had been relating, with tears of joy, how Sintram was softened by the presence of the angel Gabrielle, almost healed, and how he dared to hope that the evil dreams had yielded. And now the sword, as it whizzed round the furious youth, had almost wounded the good old man.

Rolf stopped short, and clasping his hand, he said, with a deep sigh, "Alas, Sintram, my foster-child, darling of my heart, what has come over you, stirring you fearfully to rage?"

The youth stood awhile, as if spellbound. He looked

into his old friend's face with a fixed and melancholy gaze, and his eyes became dim, like expiring watch fires seen through a thick cloud of mist.

At length, he sighed forth these words, almost inaudibly, "Good Rolf, good Rolf, depart from me! Your garden of Heaven is no home for me. And, if sometimes, a light breeze blows open its golden gates, so that I can look in and see the flowery meadowland where the dear angels dwell, then straightway, between them and me, the cold north wind and the icy storm come, and the sounding doors fly together, and I remain outside, lonely, in endless winter."

"Beloved young knight, oh, listen to me. Listen to the good angel within you! Do you not bear in your hand that very sword with which the pure lady girded[8] you? Does not her scarf wave over your raging breast? Do you not recollect how you used to say, that no man could wish for more than had fallen to you?"

"Yes, Rolf, I have said that," replied Sintram, sinking on the mossy turf, bitterly weeping; tears also ran over the old man's white beard.

Before long, the youth stood again erect, his tears ceased to flow, his looks were fearful, cold, and grim, and he said, "You see, Rolf, I have passed blessed peaceful days, and I thought that the powers of evil would never again have dominion over me. Perhaps, it might have been, as day would ever be, did the Sun ever stand in the sky. But ask the poor Earth, overtaken by night, for which reason she looks so dark! Bid her again smile, as she was accustomed to do!

"Old man, she cannot smile, and now that the gentle compassionate Moon has disappeared behind the clouds with her only funeral veil, she cannot even weep. And, in this hour of darkness, all that is wild and mad wakes up. So, stop me not, I tell you, stop me not! Hurrah, behind the pale Moon!" His voice changed to a hoarse murmur at these last words, storm-like. He tore away from the trembling old man, and rushed through the forest. Rolf knelt down and prayed, and wept silently.

CHAPTER XII

How Sintram Raised a Tempest

WHERE the beach was wildest and the cliffs most steep and rugged, where the remains of three shattered oaks, perhaps marking where human victims had been sacrificed in heathen times, rose close by, there now stood Sintram, leaning, as if exhausted, on his drawn sword, and gazing intently on the dancing waves.

The moon had again shone forth; and, as her pale beams fell on his motionless figure through the quivering branches of the trees, he might have been taken for some fearful idol-image.

Suddenly someone on the left half raised himself out of the high-withered grass, uttered a faint groan, and again lay down. Then between the two companions began this strange talk:

"You, who moves so strangely in the grass, do you belong to the living or to the dead?"

"As one may take it – I am dead to heaven and joy, and I live for hell and anguish."

"It seems to me that I have heard you before."

"Oh, yes."

"Are you a troubled spirit? And was your life-blood poured out here during times of old in sacrifice to idols?"

"I am a troubled spirit, but no man ever has, or ever can, shed my blood. I have been cast down into a frightful abyss!"

"Did you there break your neck?"

"I live, and shall live longer than you."

"Almost, you seem to me, the Crazy Pilgrim with the dead men's bones."

"I am not he, though often we are companions. Aye, we walk together, right near and friendly. But to you, it must be said, he thinks me mad. If sometimes I urge him, and say to him, 'Take!' then he hesitates and points upwards towards the stars. And if I say, 'Take not!' then, without doubt, he seizes on it in some awkward manner and so spoils my best joys and pleasures. But, in spite of this, we remain, in some measure, brothers-in-arms, and, indeed, all but kinsmen."

"Give me your hand, and let me help you to get up."

"That might bring you no good, my active young sir. In truth, you have already helped to raise me. Give heed awhile."

Wilder and ever wilder were the struggles on the ground. Thick clouds hurried over the moon and the stars, on a long unknown wild journey, and Sintram's thoughts grew no less wild and stormy, while far and near an awful howling could be heard amidst the trees and the grass.

At length, the mysterious being arose from the ground. As if with a fearful curiosity, the moon, through a rent in the clouds, cast a beam upon Sintram's companion, and made clear to the shuddering youth that the Little Master stood by him.

"Go away!" cried he, "I will not listen anymore to your evil stories about the Knight Paris. They would end by driving me quite mad."

"My stories about Paris are not needed for that!" the Little Master grinned. "It is enough that the Helen of your heart should be journeying towards Montfaucon. Believe me, madness has you already — head and heart. Or would you that she should remain? For that, however, you must be more courteous to me than you are now." In addition, he raised his voice towards the sea, as if fiercely rebuking it, so that Sintram could not but shudder and tremble before the dwarf.

But Sintram checked himself and, grasping his sword-hilt with both hands, he said, contemptuously, "You and Gabrielle! What acquaintance do you have with Gabrielle?"

"Not much," was the reply, and the Little Master might be seen to quake with fear and rage as he continued, "I cannot bear the name of your Helen. Do not yell it in my ears ten times in a breath. What if the tempest should increase? If the waves should swell and roll on until they form a foaming ring round the whole coast of Norway? The voyage to Montfaucon must, in that case, be altogether given up, and your Helen would remain here, at least through the long, long, dark winter."

"If! If!" replied Sintram, with scorn. "Is the sea your slave? Are the storms your workmen?"

"They are rebels, accursed rebels," muttered the Little Master in his red beard. "You must lend me your aid, Sir Knight, if I am to subdue them. But you do not have the heart for it."

"Boaster, evil boaster!" answered the youth. "What do you ask of me?"

"Not much, Sir Knight. Nothing at all, for one who has strength and ardour of soul. You need only look at the sea steadily and keenly for one half-hour, without ever ceasing to wish with all your might that it should foam and rage and swell, and never again rest 'til winter has laid its icy hold upon your mountains. Winter is enough to hinder King Menelaus from his voyage to Montfaucon. And now give me a lock of your black hair, which is blowing so wildly about your head, like ravens' or vultures' wings."

The youth drew his sharp dagger, madly cut off a lock of his hair, threw it to the strange being, and now gazed, as he desired, powerfully wishing, on the waves of the sea. And softly, quite softly, the waters stirred themselves, as one whispers in troubled dreams when one would gladly rest and cannot.

Sintram was on the point of giving up, when a ship, with white-swelling sails, appeared in the moonbeams, towards the south. Anguish came over him. That Gabrielle would very soon sail away. He wished again, with all his power, and fixed his eyes intently on the watery abyss.

"Sintram," a voice might have said to him, "Sintram, are you indeed the same who so lately were gazing on the moistened heaven of the eyes of Gabrielle?"

And now the waters heaved more mightily, and the howling tempest swept over the ocean. The breakers, white with foam, became visible in the moonlight. Then the Little Master threw the lock of Sintram's hair up towards the clouds, and, as it was blown to and fro by the blast of wind, the storm burst in all its fury, so that sea and sky were covered with one thick cloud, and far off might be heard the cries of distress from many a sinking vessel.

But the Crazy Pilgrim, with the dead men's bones, rose up in the midst of the waves, close to the shore, gigantic and tall, and fearfully rocking. The boat in which he stood was hidden from sight, so mightily the waves raged round about it.

"You must save him, Little Master. You must certainly save him," cried Sintram's voice, angrily entreating, through the roaring of the winds and waves.

But the dwarf replied, with a laugh, "Be quite at rest for him. He will be able to save himself. The waves can do him no harm. Do you see? They are only begging of him, and therefore they jump up so boldly round him. And he gives them bountiful charity, very bountiful, that I can assure you."

In fact, it seemed that the pilgrim threw some bones into the sea, and passed unscathed on his way.

Sintram felt his blood run cold with horror, and he

rushed wildly towards the castle. His companion had either fled or vanished away.

CHAPTER XIII

The Heartbreak of Biorn

IN the castle, Biorn, Gabrielle, and Folko of Montfaucon were sitting round the great stone table, from which, since the arrival of his noble guests, those suits of armour – formerly the established companions of the Lord of the Castle – had been removed and placed all together in a heap in the adjoining room.

At this time, while the storm was beating so furiously against doors and windows, it seemed as if the ancient armour were also stirring in the next room. Several times, Gabrielle half rose from her seat in great alarm, fixing her eyes on the small iron door, as though she expected to see an armed spectre issue from there, bending with his mighty helmet through the low vaulted doorway.

The Knight Biorn smiled grimly, and said, as if he had guessed her thoughts, "Oh, he will never again come out from that place. I have put an end to that forever."

His guests stared at him doubtingly. And with a strange air of unconcern, as though the storm had awakened all the fierceness of his soul, he began the following history:

"I was once a happy man myself. I could smile, as you do, and I could rejoice in the morning as you do. That was before the sanctimonious Chaplain had so bewildered the wise mind of my lovely wife with his pious platitudes that she went into a cloister, and left me alone with our wild boy. That was not fair treatment of the fair Verena.

"Well, so it was, that in the first days of her dawning beauty, before I knew her, many knights sought her hand. Amongst them was Sir Weigand the Slender, and towards him Verena showed that she was most favourably inclined. Her parents were well aware that Weigand's rank and station were little below their own, and that his early fame as a warrior without reproach stood high, so that – before long – Verena and he were considered as affianced.

"One day, it happened that they were walking together in the orchard, when a shepherd was driving his flock up the mountain beyond. Verena saw a little snow-white lamb frolicking gaily, and longed for it. Weigand vaulted over the railings, overtook the shepherd, and offered him two gold bracelets for the lamb. But the shepherd would not part with it, and scarcely listened to the Knight, all the while going quietly up the mountainside, with Weigand close upon him.

"At last, Weigand lost patience. He threatened, and the shepherd – sturdy and proud, like his entire race in our northern land – threatened in return. Suddenly Weigand's sword resounded upon his head. The stroke should have fallen flat, but who can control a fiery horse or a drawn sword? The bleeding shepherd, with a cloven skull, fell down the precipice, and his frightened flock bleated on the mountain.

"Only the little lamb ran, in its terror, to the orchard, pushing itself through the garden-rails and lying at Verena's feet, as if asking for help, all red with its master's blood. She took it up in her arms, and, from that moment, never suffered Weigand the Slender to appear again before her face.

"She continued to cherish the little lamb, and seemed to take pleasure in nothing else in the world, and became pale and turned towards Heaven. She would soon have taken the veil, but just then, I came to aid her father in a bloody war, and rescued him from his enemies. The old man represented this to her, and, softly smiling, she gave me her lovely hand.

"His grief would not suffer the unhappy Weigand to remain in his own country. It drove him forth as a pilgrim to Asia, where our forefathers came, and there he did wonderful deeds, both of valour and self-abasement. Truly, my heart was strangely weak when I heard him spoken of at that time.

"After some years he returned, and wished to build a church or monastery on that mountain towards the west, where the walls of my castle are distinctly seen. It was said that he wished to become a priest there. But it occurred otherwise, for some pirates had sailed from the southern seas, and, on hearing of the building of this monastery, their Chief thought to find much gold belonging to the lord of the castle and to the master builders. Or else, if he surprised and carried them off, to extort a mighty ransom from them. He did not yet know northern courage and northern weapons, but he soon gained that knowledge.

"Having landed in the creek under the black rocks, he made his way through a by-path up to the building, surrounded it, and thought that the affair was now ended. Then out rushed Weigand and his builders, and fell upon them with swords, hatchets, and hammers. The pirates fled away to their ships, with Weigand behind to take vengeance on them.

"In passing by our castle, he caught a sight of Verena on the terrace, and, for the first time during so many years, she bestowed a courteous and kind salutation on the glowing victor. At that moment, a dagger, hurled by one of the pirates in the midst of his hasty flight, struck Weigand's uncovered head and he fell to the ground bleeding and insensible.

"We completed the rout of the pirates, then I had the wounded knight brought into the castle, and my pale Verena glowed as lilies in the light of the morning sun, and Weigand opened his eyes with a smile when he was brought near her. He refused to be taken into any room but the small one close to this where the armour is now placed, for he said that he felt as if it were alike the cell that he soon hoped to inhabit in his quiet cloister.

"All was done according to his wish. My sweet Verena nursed him, and he appeared at first to be on the straightest road to recovery, but his head continued weak and liable to confusion by the slightest emotion, his walk was rather a falling than a walking, and his cheeks were colourless. We could not let him go.

"When we were sitting here together in the evening, he used to come tottering into the hall through the low doorway, and my heart was sad, and wrathful too, when the soft eyes of Verena beamed so sweetly on him, and a glow like that of the evening sky hovered over her lily cheeks. But I bore it, and I could have borne it to the end of our lives, when Verena went into a cloister!"

His head fell so heavily onto his folded hands, that the stone table seemed to groan beneath it, and he remained a long while, motionless as a corpse.

When he again raised himself up, his eyes glared fearfully as he looked round the hall, and he said to Folko, "Your beloved Hamburgers, Gotthard Lenz, and his son Rudlieb, they have much to answer for! Who bid them to come and be shipwrecked so close to my castle?"

Folko cast a piercing look on him, and a fearful inquiry was on the point of escaping his lips when another look at the trembling Gabrielle made him silent, at least for the present moment, and the Knight Biorn continued his narrative.

"Verena was with her nuns. I was left alone, and throughout the day, my despair had driven me through forest, brook, and mountain. In the twilight, I returned to my deserted castle, and I scarcely was in the hall when the little door creaked, and Weigand, who had slept through everything, crept towards me, and asked, 'Where can Verena be?'

"Then I became mad, and howled at him, 'She has gone mad, and so have I, and you also, and now we are all mad!' Merciful Heaven, the wound on his head burst open, and a dark stream flowed over his face – how different from the redness when Verena met him at the castle-gate – and he rushed forth, raving mad, into the wilderness outside, and he has wandered all around as a crazy pilgrim ever since."

Biorn was silent, and so were Folko and Gabrielle, all three pale and cold, like images of the dead. At length, the fearful narrator added in a low voice, as if he was quite exhausted, "He has visited me since that time, but he will never again come through the little door. Have I not established peace and order in my castle?"

CHAPTER XIV

The Baron Seeks Reparation

SINTRAM had not returned home, when those of the castle took themselves to rest, in deep bewilderment. No one thought of him, for every heart was filled with strange forebodings, and with uncertain cares. Even the heroic breast of the Knight of Montfaucon heaved in doubt.

Old Rolf remained outside still, weeping in the forest, heedless of the storm that beat on his unprotected head, while he waited for his young master. But he had journeyed a different way; and when the morning dawned, he entered the castle from the opposite side.

Gabrielle's slumbers had been sweet during the whole night. It had seemed to her that angels with golden wings had blown away the wild histories of the evening before, and had wafted the bright flowers, the sparkling sea, and the green hills of her own home to her. She smiled, and drew her breath, calmly and softly, whilst the magical tempest raged and howled through the forests, and continued to battle with the troubled sea.

But, in truth, when she awoke in the morning, and

still heard the rattling of the windows, and saw the clouds still hiding the face of the heavens, she could have wept with anxiety and sadness, especially when she heard from her maidens that Folko had already left their apartment clad in full armour, as if prepared for combat. At the same time, she heard the sound of the heavy tread of armed men in the echoing halls, and, on inquiring, found that the Knight of Montfaucon had assembled all his retainers to be in readiness to protect their lady.

Wrapped in a cloak of ermine, she stood trembling as a tender flower just sprung up through the snow, tottering beneath a winter's storm. Then Sir Folko entered the room, in all his shining armour, peacefully carrying his golden helmet with the long shadowy plumes in his hand. He saluted Gabrielle with cheerful serenity, and at a sign from him, her attendants retired, while the men-at-arms outside were heard quietly dispersing.

"Lady," said he, as he took his seat beside her, on a couch to which he led her, already reassured by his presence. "Lady, will you forgive your knight for having left you to endure some moments of anxiety? But honour and stern justice called him. Now all is set in order, quietly and peacefully. Dismiss your fears and every thought that has troubled you, as things which are no more."

"But you and Biorn?" asked Gabrielle.

"On the word of a knight," replied he, "all is well there." And then he began to discuss indifferent subjects with his usual ease and wit.

But Gabrielle, bending towards him, said with deep

emotion, "Oh, Folko, my knight, the flower of my life, my protector and my dearest hope on earth, tell me all, if you may. But if a promise binds you, it is different. You know that I am of the race of Portamour, and I would ask nothing from my knight which could cast even a breath of suspicion on his spotless shield."

Folko thought gravely for one instant, then looking at her with a bright smile, he said, "It is not that, Gabrielle, but can you bear what I have to disclose? Will you not sink down under it, as a slender fir gives way under a mass of snow?"

She raised herself somewhat proudly, and said, "I have already reminded you of the name of my father's house. Let me now add, that I am the wedded wife of the Baron of Montfaucon."

"Then so let it be," replied Folko solemnly. "And if that which should have remained hidden in the darkness — a deed which belongs to those of wickedness — must come forth into the open, at least let it come forth less fearfully with a sudden flash. Know then, Gabrielle, that the wicked knight who would have slain my friends Gotthard and Rudlieb is none other than our kinsman and host, Biorn of the Fiery Eyes."

Gabrielle shuddered and covered her eyes with her fair hands. But, at the end of a moment, she looked up with a bewildered air, and said, "I have heard wrong surely — although it is true that yesterday evening such a thought struck me — for did not you say, awhile ago, that all was settled and at peace between you and Biorn? Between you, brave Baron, and such a man, after such a crime?"

"You heard right," answered Folko, looking with fond delight on the delicate yet high-minded lady. "This morning, with the earliest dawn, I went to him and challenged him to a mortal combat in the neighbouring valley, if he were the man whose castle had almost become an altar of sacrifice to Gotthard and Rudlieb. He was already completely armed, and merely saying, 'I am he,' and he followed me to the forest.

"But when he stood alone at the place of combat, he flung his shield away, down an unstable precipice. Then he hurled his sword after it, and next – with gigantic strength – he tore off his coat of mail, and said, 'Now, attack, you minister of vengeance, for I am a heavy sinner, and I dare not fight with you.' How could I then attack him? And so, a strange truce was agreed on between us.

"He is half as my vassal, and yet I solemnly forgave him in my own name and in that of my friends. He was contrite, and yet no tear was in his eye, no gentle word on his lips. He is only kept under by the power with which I am endowed by having right on my side, and it is on that tenure that Biorn is my vassal.

"I know not, lady, whether you can bear to see us together on these terms. If not, I will ask for hospitality in some other castle, for this wild autumnal storm may put off our voyage for many a day. There are no castles in Norway which would not receive us joyfully and honourably, only I think that if we depart directly, and in such a manner, the heart of this savage man will break."

"Where my noble lord remains, there I also remain joyfully under his protection," replied Gabrielle, and again

her heart glowed with rapture at the greatness of her
knight.

CHAPTER XV

The Appearance of Sintram

THE noble lady had just unbuckled her knight's armour with her own fair hands – on the field of battle, pages or esquires alone were bidden to handle Montfaucon's armour – and now she was throwing his mantle of blue velvet, embroidered with gold, over his shoulders, when the door opened gently, and Sintram entered the room, humbly greeting them.

Gabrielle received him kindly, as was her custom, but she suddenly turned pale, looked away, and said, "Oh, Sintram, what has happened to you? And how can one single night have altered you so fearfully?"

Sintram stood still, thunderstruck, and feeling as if he himself did not know what had befallen him. Then Folko took him by the hand, led him towards a bright polished shield, and said very earnestly, "Look here at yourself, young knight!"

At the first glance, Sintram drew back horrified. He fancied that he saw the Little Master before him, with that single upright feather sticking out of his cap; but, at length, he perceived that the mirror was only showing him his own image and none other, and that his own wild use of his dagger had given him this strange and spectre-like aspect.

"Who has done that to you?" asked Folko, yet more grave and solemn. "And what terror makes your disordered hair stand on end?"

Sintram knew not what answer to give. He felt as if a judgment were coming on him, and a shameful degrading from his knightly rank.

Suddenly, Folko drew him away from the shield, and taking him towards the rattling window, he asked, "From where does this tempest come?"

Still, Sintram kept silent and his limbs began to tremble under him.

Gabrielle, pale and terrified, whispered, "Oh, Folko, my knight, what has happened? Oh, tell me, have we come into an enchanted castle?"

"The land of our northern ancestors," Folko replied with solemnity, "is full of mysterious knowledge. But, for all that, we may not call its people enchanters. Still, this youth has cause to watch himself carefully. He whom the evil one has touched by as much as one hair on his head …"

Sintram heard no more. With a deep groan, he staggered out of the room.

As he left it, he met old Rolf, still almost numb from the cold and storms of the night. Now, in his joy at seeing his young master again, he did not remark on Sintram's altered appearance; but, as he accompanied him to his sleeping room, he said, "Witches and spirits of the tempest must have taken up their abode on the seashore. I am certain that such wild storms never arise without some devilish arts."

Sintram fell into a fainting-fit from which Rolf was able, with difficulty, to revive him sufficiently so that he could appear in the Great Hall at the midday hour. However, before he went down, Sintram asked for a shield to be brought. He saw himself within, and cut close round his head – in grief and horror – the rest of his long black hair, so that he made himself look almost like a monk; and in such a manner he joined the others already assembled round the table.

They all looked at him with surprise, but old Biorn rose up and said fiercely, "Are you going to take yourself to a cloister, in addition to the fair lady, your mother?"

A commanding look from the Baron of Montfaucon checked any further outburst; and, as if in apology, Biorn added, with a forced smile, "I was only wondering if any accident had befallen him, like Absalom's, and if he had been obliged to save himself from being strangled by parting with all of his hair."

"You should not jest with holy things," answered the Baron severely, and all were silent.

No sooner was the repast ended, than Folko and Gabrielle, with a grave and courteous salutation, retired to their apartments.

CHAPTER XVI

The Entertainments of Winter

FROM this time, life in the castle took quite a different form. Those two bright beings, Folko and Gabrielle, spent most part of the day in their apartments, and when they showed themselves, it was with quiet dignity and grave silence, while Biorn and Sintram stood before them in humble fear.

Nevertheless, Biorn could not bear the thought of his guests seeking shelter in any other knight's abode. When Folko once spoke of it, something like a tear stood in the wild man's eye. His head sank, and he said softly, "As you please. But I feel that if you go, I shall run among the rocks for days."

Thus, they all remained together; for the storm continued to rage with such increasing fury over the sea, that no sea voyage could be thought of, and the oldest man in Norway could not call to mind such an autumn. The priests examined all the runic books, the bards looked through their lays and tales, and yet they could find no record of the like.

Biorn and Sintram braved the tempest; but, during the few hours in which Folko and Gabrielle showed themselves, the father and son were always in the castle, as if respectfully waiting upon them; the rest of the day – nay, often through whole nights – they rushed through the forests and over the rocks in pursuit of bears.

Meanwhile, Folko called up all the brightness of his fancy, all his courtly grace, in order to make Gabrielle forget that she was living in this wild castle, and that the long, hard northern winter was setting in, which would ice them in for many a month.

Sometimes he would relate bright tales; then he would play the liveliest tunes to induce Gabrielle to lead a dance with her attendants; then, again, handing his lute to one of the women, he would take a part in the dance, knowing well how to express his devotion to his lady by that means. Another time, he would have the spacious halls of the castle prepared for his armed retainers to go through their warlike exercises, and Gabrielle always adjudged the reward to the conqueror. Folko often joined the circle of combatants, but only so that he met their attacks, defending himself, thereby depriving no one of the prize.

The Norwegians, who stood around as spectators, used to compare him to the god Balder, one of the heroes of their old traditions, who was in the habit of letting the darts of his companions be hurled against him, conscious that he was invulnerable, and of his own supernatural strength.

At the close of one of these martial exercises, old Rolf advanced towards Folko, and beckoning him with a humble look, said softly, "They call you the beautiful mighty Balder – and they are right. But even the beautiful mighty Balder did not escape death. Take heed."

Folko looked at him, wondering.

"Not that I know of any treachery," the old man continued, "or that I can even foresee the likelihood of any – God keep a Norwegian from such a fear! But when you stand before me, in all the brightness of your glory, the fleetingness of everything earthly weighs down on my mind, and I cannot refrain from saying, 'Take heed, noble Baron! Oh, take heed! Even the most beautiful glory comes to an end.'"

"Those are wise and pious thoughts," replied Folko calmly, "and I will treasure them in a pure heart."

The good Rolf was often with Folko and Gabrielle, and made a connecting link between the two widely differing parties in the castle. For how could he have ever forsaken his own Sintram! Only in the wild hunting expeditions through the howling storms and tempests was he no longer able to follow his young lord.

At length, the icy reign of winter began in all its glory. On this account, a return to Normandy was impossible, and therefore the magical storm was lulled. The hills and valleys shone brilliantly in their white attire of snow, and Folko used sometimes, with skates on his feet, to draw his lady in a light sledge over the glittering frozen lakes and streams. On the other hand, the bear-hunts of the Lord of the Castle and his son took on a still more desperate and, to them, joyous course.

About this time – when Christmas was drawing

near, and Sintram was seeking to overpower his dread of the awful dreams by the most daring expeditions – Folko and Gabrielle stood together on one of the terraces of the castle. The evening was mild. The snow-clad fields were glowing in the red light of the setting sun. From below, there were heard men's voices singing songs of ancient heroic times, while they worked in the armourer's forge.

At last, the songs died away, the beating of hammers ceased, and, without the speakers being seen, or there being any possibility of distinguishing them by their voices, the following discourse arose:

"Who is the bravest amongst all those whose race derives its origin from our renowned land?"

"It is Folko of Montfaucon."

"Rightly said, but, tell me, is there anything from which even this bold Baron draws back?"

"In truth, there is one thing, and we, who have never left Norway, face it quite willingly and joyfully."

"And that is –?"

"A bear-hunt in winter, over trackless plains of snow, down frightful ice-covered precipices."

"Truly, you answer correctly, my comrade. He who knows not how to fasten our skates on his feet, how to turn in them to the right or left at a moment's warning, he may be a valiant knight in other respects, but he had better keep away from our hunting parties, and remain with his timid wife in her apartments."

At which, the speakers were heard to laugh, well pleased, and then to take themselves again to their armourer's work.

Folko stood, long buried in thought. A glow, beyond that of the evening sky, reddened his cheek. Gabrielle also remained silent, considering she knew not what. At last, she took courage, and embracing her beloved, she said, "Tomorrow, you will go forth to hunt the bear, will you not? And you will bring the spoils of the chase to your lady?"

The Knight gave a joyful sign of assent, and the rest of the evening was spent in dances and music.

CHAPTER XVII

Undertaking a Bear Hunt

"SEE, my noble Lord," said Sintram the next morning, when Folko had expressed his wish to go with him, "these skates of ours give such wings to our course that we go down the mountainside as swiftly as the wind. Even in going up again, we are too quick for anyone to be able to pursue us, and on the plains, no horse can keep up with us. Yet, they can only be worn with safety by those who are well practised. It seems as though some strange spirit dwells in them, which is fearfully dangerous to any that have not learnt the management of them in their childhood."

Folko answered, somewhat proudly, "Do you suppose that this is the first time that I have been amongst your mountains? Years ago I joined in this sport, and, thank Heaven, there is no knightly exercise which does not speedily become familiar to me."

Sintram did not venture to make any further objections, and still less did old Biorn. They both felt relieved when they saw with what skill and ease Folko buckled the skates on his feet, without suffering anyone to assist him. This day they hunted up the mountain in pursuit of a fierce bear, which had often escaped from them.

Before long, it was necessary that they should separate, and Sintram offered himself as companion to Folko, who, touched by the humble manner of the youth and his devotion to him, forgot all that had latterly seemed mysterious in the pale altered being before him, and agreed heartily.

As they continued to climb higher and higher up the mountain, and saw from many a giddy height the rocks and crags below them looking like a vast expanse of sea suddenly turned into ice whilst tossed by a violent tempest, the noble Montfaucon drew his breath more freely. He poured forth war-songs and love-longs in the clear mountain air, and the startled echoes repeated from rock to rock the lays of his Frankish home. He sprang lightly from one precipice to another, strongly using his staff for support, and turning to the right or to the left, as the fancy seized him.

The Baron's skill was so apparent that Sintram was compelled to exchange his former anxiety for a wondering admiration, and the hunters, whose eyes had never left the Baron, burst forth with loud applause, proclaiming fresh glory of their guest far and wide.

The good fortune, which usually accompanied Folko's deeds of arms, still seemed unwilling to leave him; after a short search, he and Sintram found distinct traces of the savage animal, and, with beating hearts, they followed the track so swiftly that even a winged enemy would have been unable to escape from them.

But the creature whom they sought did not attempt to take flight – he lay sulkily in a cavern near the top of a steep precipitous rock, infuriated by the shouts of the hunters, and only waiting in his lazy fury for someone to be bold enough to climb up to his retreat, that he might tear him to pieces.

Folko and Sintram had now reached the foot of this rock, the rest of the hunters being dispersed over the far-extending plain. The track led the two companions up the rock, and they set about climbing on the opposite sides of it, that they might be the surer of not missing their prey.

Folko reached the lonely topmost point first, and cast his eyes around. A wide, boundless tract of country, covered with pristine snow, was spread before him, melting in the distance into the lowering clouds of the gloomy evening sky. He almost thought that he must have missed the traces of the fearful beast, when close beside him, from a cleft in the rock, issued a long growl, and a huge black bear appeared on the snow, standing on its hind legs and, with glaring eyes, it advanced towards the Baron.

Sintram, meanwhile, was struggling in vain to make his way up the rock against the masses of snow continually slipping down.

Joyful at a combat so long untried as almost to be new, Folko of Montfaucon levelled his hunting spear, and awaited the attack of the wild beast. He suffered it to approach so near that its fearful claws were almost upon him, then he made a thrust, and the spear-head was buried deep in the bear's breast.

However, the furious beast still pressed on with a fierce growl, kept up on its hind legs by the cross iron of the spear, and the knight was forced to plant his feet deep in the earth to resist the savage assault. Before him, ever closer, came the grim and bloody face of the bear, and close in his ear, its deep savage growl, wrung forth partly by the agony of death, partly by thirst for blood.

At length, the bear's resistance grew weaker, and the dark blood streamed freely upon the snow. He tottered, and one powerful thrust hurled him backwards over the edge of the precipice. At the same instant, Sintram stood by the Baron of Montfaucon. Folko said, drawing a deep breath, "But I have not yet the prize in my hands, and have it I must, since fortune has given me a claim to it. Look, one of my skates seems to be out of order. Do you think that it will hold enough to slide down to the foot of the precipice?"

"Let me go instead," said Sintram. "I will bring you the head and the claws of the bear."

"A true knight," replied Folko, with some displeasure, "never does a knightly deed by halves. What I ask is, whether my skate will hold?"

As Sintram bent down to look, and was on the point of saying, "No!" he suddenly heard a voice close to him, saying, "Why, yes, to be sure. There is no doubt about it."

Folko thought that Sintram had spoken, and slid down with the swiftness of an arrow, whilst his companion looked up in great surprise – the hated form of the Little Master met his eyes. As he was going to address him with angry words, he heard the sound of the Baron's fearful fall, and he stood still in silent horror.

There was a breathless silence also in the abyss below.

"Now, why do you delay?" said the Little Master, after a pause. "He is dashed to pieces. Go back to the castle, and take the fair Helen for yourself."

Sintram shuddered. Then his hateful companion began to praise Gabrielle's charms in so glowing and deceiving words that the heart of the youth swelled with emotions he had never before known. He only thought of him who was now lying at the foot of the rock as an obstacle, one between him and Heaven that now had to be removed, and he turned towards the castle.

But a cry was heard below, "Help! Help! My comrade! I am yet alive, but I am sorely wounded."

Sintram's will changed, and he called to the Baron, "I am coming."

But the Little Master said, "Nothing can be done to help King Menelaus, and the fair Helen knows it already. She is only waiting for the Knight Paris to comfort her." And, with detestable craft, he wove the tale of the Judgment of Paris in with what was actually happening, including the most highly fashioned praises of the lovely Gabrielle, and – alas – the dazzled youth yielded to him and fled!

Again, Sintram heard far off the Baron's voice calling to him, "Knight Sintram, Knight Sintram, you on whom I bestowed the holy order, haste to me and help me! The she-bear and her whelps will be upon me, and I cannot use my right arm! Knight Sintram, Knight Sintram, haste to help me!"

The Baron's cries were overpowered by the furious speed with which the two were carried along on their skates, and by the evil words of the Little Master, who was mocking the late proud bearing of King Menelaus towards the poor Sintram.

At last, the Little Master shouted, "Good luck to you, she-bear! Good luck to your whelps! There is a glorious meal for you! Now you will feed upon the fear of Heathendom, him at whose name Moorish brides weep — the mighty Baron of Montfaucon. Never again, dainty knight, will you shout at the head of your troops, 'Mountjoy St. Denys!'[9]"

However, scarcely had this holy name passed the lips of the Little Master, when he set up a howl of anguish, writhing with horrible contortions, and wringing his hands, which ended by his disappearance in a storm of snow, which then arose.

Sintram planted his staff firmly in the ground, and stopped. How strangely did the wide expanse of snow, the distant mountains rising above it, and the dark green fir-woods look at him in cold reproachful silence! He felt as if he would sink under the weight of his sorrow and his guilt.

The bell of a distant hermitage came floating sadly over the plain, and with a burst of tears, he exclaimed, as the darkness grew thicker round him, "My mother! My mother! I once had a beloved tender mother, and she said I was a good child!" A ray of comfort came to him, as if brought on an angel's wing – perhaps Montfaucon was not yet dead! And he flew like lightning along the path, back to the steep rock.

When he got to the fearful place, he stooped and looked anxiously down the precipice. The moon, just ascended to full majesty, helped him; the Knight of Montfaucon, pale and bleeding, was half kneeling against the rock. His right arm, crushed in his fall, hung powerless at his side, and it was plain that he could not draw his good sword out of the scabbard. Nevertheless, he was keeping the bear and her young ones at bay by his bold threatening looks, so that they only crept round him, growling angrily, ready to attack at any moment, but often driven back, frightened, at the majestic air by which the Baron conquered, even when defenceless.

"Oh! What a hero would have perished!" groaned Sintram. "And through whose guilt?" In an instant, Sintram's spear flew with so true an aim that the bear fell, writhing in her blood. The young ones ran away, howling.

The Baron looked up with surprise. His countenance beamed as the light of the moon fell upon it, grave and stern yet mild, like some angelic vision. "Come down!" he beckoned; and Sintram slid down the side of the precipice, full of anxious haste.

Sintram was going to attend to the wounded man, but Folko said, "First cut off the head and claws of the bear which I slew. I promised to bring the spoils of the chase to my lovely Gabrielle. Then come to me, and bind up my wounds. My right arm is broken."

Sintram obeyed the Baron's commands. When the tokens of victory had been secured, and the broken arm bound up, Folko desired the youth to help him back to the castle.

"Oh, Heavens!" said Sintram in a low voice. "If I dared to look into your face! Or only knew how to come near you!"

"You were indeed going forward on an evil course," said Montfaucon, gravely. "But how could we, any of us, stand before God, did not repentance help us? At any rate, you have now saved my life, and let that thought cheer your heart."

The youth, with tenderness and strength, supported the Baron's left arm, and they both went their way silently in the moonlight.

CHAPTER XVIII

The Consequences of the Hunt

SOUNDS of wailing were heard from the castle as they approached. The chapel was solemnly lit up; and within it, knelt Gabrielle, lamenting for the death of the Knight of Montfaucon.

But how quickly all changed, when the noble Baron, pale and bleeding, yet having escaped all mortal danger, stood smiling at the entrance of the holy building, and said, in a low, gentle voice, "Look up, Gabrielle, and be not afraid. For, by the honour of my race, your knight still lives."

Oh! With what joy did Gabrielle's eyes sparkle, as she turned to her knight, and then raised them again to Heaven, still streaming, but from the deep source of thankful joy!

With the help of two pages, Folko knelt down beside her, and they both sanctified their happiness with a silent prayer.

When they left the chapel, the wounded knight being

tenderly supported by his lady, Sintram was standing outside in the darkness, himself as gloomy as the night, and, like a bird of the night, shunning the sight of men. Yet, he came trembling forward into the torchlight, laid the bear's head and claws at the feet of Gabrielle, and said, "The noble Folko of Montfaucon presents the spoils of today's chase to his lady."

The Norwegians burst forth with shouts of joyful surprise at the stranger knight, who in his very first hunting expedition had slain the most fearful and dangerous beast of their mountains.

Then Folko looked around, with a smile, as he said, "And now none of you must jeer at me, if I stay at home for a short time with my timid wife."

Those, who the day before had talked together in the armourer's forge, came out from the crowd, and bowing low, they replied, "Noble Baron, who could have thought that there was any knightly exercise in the whole world in the which you would not show yourself far above all other men?"

"The pupil of old Sir Hugh may be somewhat trusted," answered Folko kindly. "But now, you bold northern warriors, bestow some praises also on my deliverer, who saved me from the claws of the she-bear when I was leaning against the rock, wounded by my fall." He pointed to Sintram, and the general shout was again raised; and old Rolf, with tears of joy in his eyes, bent his head over his foster-son's hand.

But Sintram drew back shuddering. "Did you but know whom you see before you," he said, "all of your spears would be aimed at my heart, and perhaps that would be the best thing for me. But I spare the honour of my father and of his race, and at this time, I will not confess. Only this much you must know, noble warriors –"

"Young man," interrupted Folko, with a reproving look, "already again so wild and fierce? I desire that you will hold your peace about your dreaming fancies."

Sintram was silenced for a moment; but hardly had Folko begun smilingly to move towards the steps of the castle, when Sintram cried out, "Oh, no, noble wounded knight, stay yet awhile. I will serve you in everything that your heart can desire, but in this circumstance, I cannot serve you.

"Brave warriors, you must and shall know as much as this. I am no longer worthy to live under the same roof with the noble Baron of Montfaucon and his angelic wife, Gabrielle. And you, my aged father, goodnight. Do not long for me. I intend to live in the stone fortress on the Rocks of the Moon, 'til a change of some kind comes over me."

Present in his way of speaking was that something against which no one dared to set himself, not even Folko. The wild Biorn bowed his head humbly, and said, "Do according to your pleasure, my poor son, for I fear that you are right."

Then Sintram walked solemnly and silently through the castle-gate, followed by the good Rolf, while Gabrielle led her exhausted lord up to their apartments.

CHAPTER XIX

The Rocks of the Moon

THE journey on which the youth and his aged foster-father travelled towards the Rocks of the Moon, through the wild tangled paths of the snow-clad valleys, was a mournful one. From time to time, Rolf sang some verses of hymns, in which comfort and peace were promised to the penitent sinner, and Sintram thanked him for them with looks of grateful sadness. However, neither of them spoke a word else.

At length, when the dawn of day was approaching, Sintram broke the silence by saying, "Who are those two sitting over there by the frozen stream – a tall man and a little one? Their own wild hearts must have driven them also forth into the wilderness. Rolf, do you know them? The sight of them makes me shudder."

"Sir," answered the old man, "your disturbed mind deceives you. There stands a lofty fir-tree, and the old weather-beaten stump of an oak, half-covered with snow, which gives them a somewhat strange appearance. There are no men sitting by the stream."

"But, Rolf, look there! Look again carefully! Now they move, they whisper together."

"Sir, the morning breeze moves the branches, and whistles in the sharp pine-leaves and in the yellow oak-leaves, and rustles the crisp snow."

"Rolf, now they are both coming towards us. Now they are standing before us, quite close."

"Sir, it is we who get nearer to them as we walk on, and the setting moon throws such long giant-like shadows over the plain."

"Good evening!" said a hollow voice; and Sintram knew it was the Crazy Pilgrim, near to whom stood the malignant Little Master, looking more hideous than ever.

"You are right, Sir Knight," whispered Rolf, as he drew back behind Sintram, and made the Sign of the Cross on his breast and his forehead.

The bewildered youth, however, advanced towards the two figures, and said, "You have always taken wonderful pleasure in being my companions. What do you expect will come of it? And do you choose now to go with me to the stone fortress? There I will tend you, poor pale pilgrim. As for you, frightful Master, most evil dwarf, I will make you shorter by the head, to reward you for your deeds yesterday."

"That would be a fine thing," the Little Master sneered. "And perhaps you imagine that you would be doing a great service to the whole world? And, indeed, who knows? Something might be gained by it! Only, poor wretch, you cannot do it."

The pilgrim, meanwhile, was waving his pale head back and forth thoughtfully, saying, "I truly believe that you would willingly have me, and I would willingly go to you, but I may not yet. Have patience awhile. You will surely see me come, but at a distant time. First we must again visit your father together, and then you will also learn to call me by my true name, my poor friend."

"Beware of disappointing me again!" said the Little Master to the pilgrim in a threatening voice.

However, the pilgrim, pointing with his long shrivelled hand towards the Sun, which was just now rising, said, "Stop that sun or me, if you can!"

Then the first rays fell on the snow, and the Little Master ran, muttering, down a precipice; but the pilgrim walked onwards in the bright beams, calmly and with great solemnity, towards a neighbouring castle on the mountain. It was not long before its chapel-bell was heard tolling for the dead.

"For Heaven's sake," whispered the good Rolf to his knight. "What companions you have, Sir Sintram! One of them cannot bear the light of God's blessed sun, and the other has no sooner set foot in a dwelling than tidings of death wail after his track. Could he have been a murderer?"

"I do not think that to be so," said Sintram. "He has always seemed the better of the two to me. Yet it is a strange wilfulness of his not to come with me. Did I not invite him kindly? I believe that he can sing well, and he could have sung some gentle lullaby to me. Since my mother has lived in a cloister, no one sings lullabies to me anymore." At this tender recollection, his eyes moistened with tears; but he did not know what he had said, for there was wildness and confusion in his spirit.

They arrived at the Rocks of the Moon, and mounted up to the stone fortress. The Castellan[10] – an old gloomy man, the more devoted to the young Knight owing to his dark melancholy and wild deeds – hastened to lower the drawbridge. Greetings were exchanged in silence, and in silence Sintram entered, and those joyless gates closed with a crash behind the future recluse.

CHAPTER XX

The Castellan Reveals His Identity

YES, truly, a recluse, or at least something like it, did poor Sintram now become! For, towards the time of the approaching Christmas festival, his fearful dreams came over him, and seized him so fiercely that all the esquires and servants fled with shrieks out of the castle, and would never venture back again. No one remained with him except Rolf and the old Castellan.

After a while, indeed, Sintram became calm, but he went about looking so pallid and still that he might have been taken for a wandering corpse. No comforting of the good Rolf, no devout soothing lays, were of any avail; and the Castellan, with his fierce scarred features, his head almost entirely bald from a huge sword-cut, his stubborn silence, seemed like a darker shadow of the miserable Knight.

Rolf often thought of going to summon the holy Chaplain of Drontheim, but how could he have left his lord alone with the gloomy Castellan, a man who at all times raised in him a secret horror? Biorn had long had this wild strange warrior in his service, and honoured him on account of his unshaken fidelity and his fearless courage, though neither the knight nor anyone else knew where the Castellan came from, nor, indeed, exactly who he was. Very few people knew by what name to call him, but that was needless since he never entered into discourse with anyone. He was the Castellan of the stone fortress on the Rocks of the Moon, and nothing more. Rolf committed his deep heartfelt cares to the merciful God, trusting that he would soon come to his aid; and the merciful God did not fail him.

On Christmas Eve, the bell at the drawbridge sounded, and Rolf, looking over the battlements, saw the Chaplain of Drontheim standing there, with a companion indeed that surprised him – for close beside him appeared the Crazy Pilgrim, and the dead men's bones on his dark mantle shone very strangely in the glimmering starlight.

Nevertheless, the sight of the Chaplain filled the good Rolf too full of joy to leave room for any doubt in his mind; for, thought he, whoever comes with him cannot but be welcome! Therefore, he let them both in with respectful haste, and ushered them up to the hall, where Sintram, pale and with a fixed look, was sitting under the light of one flickering lamp. Rolf was obliged to support and assist the Crazy Pilgrim up the stairs, for he was quite numbed by the cold.

"I bring you a greeting from your mother," the Chaplain said as he came in; and immediately a sweet smile passed over the young Knight's countenance, and its deadly pallidness gave place to a bright soft glow.

"Oh, Heaven!" murmured he, "does my mother yet

live, and does she care to know anything about me?"

"She is endowed with a wonderful premonition of the future," replied the Chaplain. "All that you ought either to do or to leave undone is faithfully mirrored in various ways in her mind, during a half-waking trance. Now she knows of your deep sorrow, and she sends me, the father confessor of her convent, to comfort you, but at the same time to warn you. For, as she affirms, and as I am also inclined to think, many strange and heavy trials lie before you."

Sintram bowed towards the Chaplain and, with his arms crossed over his breast, said with a gentle smile, "Much have I been favoured – more, a thousand times more, than I could have dared to hope in my best hours – by this greeting from my mother, and your visit, Reverend Sir. And all after falling more fearfully low than I had ever fallen before. The mercy of the Lord is great. And however heavy the weight and punishment which He may send may be, I trust, with His grace, to be able to bear it."

Just then, the door opened, and the Castellan came in with a torch in his hand, the red glare of which made his face look the colour of blood. He cast a terrified glance at the Crazy Pilgrim, who had just sunk back in a swoon, and was supported on his seat and tended by Rolf; then he stared with astonishment at the Chaplain, and at last murmured, "A strange meeting! I believe that the hour for confession and reconciliation is now arrived."

"I believe so too," replied the priest, who had heard his low whisper. "This seems to be a day truly rich in grace and peace. That poor man yonder, whom I found half-frozen by the way, made a full confession to me at once before he followed me to a place of shelter. Do as he has done, my dark-browed warrior, and do not delay your good purpose for one instant."

Thereupon, the Chaplain left the room with the willing Castellan, but he turned back to say, "Sir Knight and your esquire! Take good care, in the meantime, of my sick charge."

Sintram and Rolf did according to the Chaplain's desire. And when, at length, their cordials made the pilgrim open his eyes once again, the young Knight said to him, with a friendly smile, "See now? You have come to visit me after all. Why did you refuse me when, a few nights ago, I asked you so earnestly to come? Perhaps I may have spoken wildly and hastily. Did that scare you away?"

A sudden expression of fear came over the pilgrim's countenance. Soon, though, he again looked up at Sintram with an air of gentle humility, saying, "Oh, my dear, dear Lord, I am most entirely devoted to you – only never speak to me of former passages between you and me. I am terrified whenever you do it. For, my lord, either I am mad and have forgotten all that is past, or you have met in the wood that Being whom I look upon as my very powerful twin brother."

Sintram gently laid his hand on the pilgrim's mouth, as he answered, "Say nothing more about that matter. I most willingly promise to be silent." Neither he nor old Rolf could understand what appeared to them so awful in the whole matter, but both shuddered. After a short pause, the pilgrim said, "I would rather sing you a song – a soft, comforting song. Have you a lute here?"

Rolf fetched one; and the pilgrim, half-raising himself on the couch, sang the following words:

> *When death is coming near,*
> *When thy heart shrinks in fear*
>   *And thy limbs fail,*
>
> *Then raise thy hands and pray*
> *To Him who smoothes thy way*
>   *Through the dark vale.*
>
> *Seest thou the eastern dawn,*
> *Hearst thou in the red morn*
>   *The angel's song?*
>
> *Oh, lift thy drooping head,*
> *Thou who in gloom and dread*
>   *Hast lain so long.*
>
> *Death comes to set thee free;*
> *Oh, meet him cheerily*
>   *As thy true friend,*
>
> *And all thy fears shall cease,*
> *And in eternal peace*
>   *Thy penance end.*

"Amen," said Sintram and Rolf, folding their hands; and while the last chords of the lute still resounded, the Chaplain and the Castellan came slowly and gently into the room.

"I bring a precious Christmas gift," said the priest. "After many sad years, hope of reconciliation and peace of conscience are returning to a noble disturbed mind. This concerns you, beloved pilgrim; and do you, my Sintram, with a joyful trust in God, take encouragement and example from it."

"More than twenty years ago," began the Castellan, at a sign from the Chaplain, "I was a bold shepherd, driving my flock up the mountains. A young knight, whom they called Weigand the Slender, followed me. He wanted to buy from me my favourite little lamb for his fair bride, and offered me much red gold for it. I sturdily refused. Over-bold, the youth boiled up in us both. A stroke of his sword hurled me senseless down the precipice."

"Not killed?" asked the pilgrim in a scarce audible voice.

"I am no ghost," replied the Castellan, somewhat morosely. Then, after an earnest look from the priest, he continued, more humbly, "I recovered slowly and in solitude, with the help of remedies which were easily found by me, a shepherd, in our productive valleys.

"When I came back into the world, no man knew me, with my scarred face and my now bald head. I heard a report going through the country that, on account of this deed of his, Sir Weigand the Slender had been rejected by his fair betrothed Verena, and how he had pined away, and she had wished to retire into a convent, but her father had persuaded her to marry the great knight, Biorn.

"There then came a fearful thirst for vengeance into my heart, and I disowned my name, and my kindred, and my home, and entered the service of the mighty Biorn, as a strange wild man, in order that Weigand the Slender should always remain a murderer, and that I might feed on his anguish.

"So I have fed upon it for all these long years. I have fed frightfully upon his self-imposed banishment, upon his cheerless return home, upon his madness. But today –" and hot tears gushed from his eyes "– but today God has broken the hardness of my heart. And, dear Sir Weigand, look upon yourself no more as a murderer, and say that you will forgive me, and pray for him who has done you so fearful an injury, and –"

Sobs choked his words. He fell at the feet of the pilgrim, who, with tears of joy, pressed him to his heart, in a symbol of forgiveness.

CHAPTER XXI

One Last Wish

THE joy of this hour passed from its first overpowering brightness to the calm and thoughtful aspect of daily life, and Weigand, now restored to health, laid aside the mantle adorned with dead men's bones, saying, "For my penance, I had chosen to carry these fearful remains about with me, with the thought that some of them might have belonged to him whom I had murdered.

"I therefore searched for them round about, in the deep beds of the mountain-torrents and in the high nests of the eagles and vultures. And while I was searching, I sometimes – could it have been only an illusion? – seemed to meet a being who was very like myself, but far more powerful, and yet paler and more haggard."

An imploring look from Sintram stopped the flow of his words. With a gentle smile, Weigand bowed towards him, and said, "You know now the deep, unutterably deep, sorrow which preyed upon me. My fear of you, and my yearning love for you, is no longer an enigma to your kind heart.

"For, dear youth, though you may be like your fearful father, you also have the kind and gentle heart of your mother. And its reflection brightens your pallid stern features, like the glow of a morning sky, which lights up ice-covered mountains and snowy valleys with the soft radiance of joy. But, alas! How long you have lived alone amidst your fellow-creatures! And how long since you have seen your mother, my dearly-loved Sintram!"

"I feel, too, as though a spring were gushing up in the barren wilderness," replied the youth, "and I should by chance be altogether restored. Could I but keep you long with me, and weep with you, dear lord, but I have that within me which says that you will very soon be taken from me."

"I believe, indeed," said the pilgrim, "that my late song was very nearly my last, and that it contained a prediction soon to be fully accomplished in me. But, as the soul of man is always like the thirsty ground, the more blessings God has bestowed on us, the more earnestly do we look out for new ones. So I would crave for one more before, as I hope, my blessed end. Yet, indeed, it cannot be granted me," he added, with a faltering voice, "for I feel myself too utterly unworthy of so high a gift."

"But it will be granted!" said the Chaplain, joyfully. "'He that humbles himself shall be exalted' and I fear not to take one purified of murder to receive a farewell from the holy and forgiving countenance of Verena."

Weigand stretched both his hands up towards Heaven, and an unspoken thanksgiving poured from his beaming eyes and brightened the smile that played on his lips.

Sintram looked sorrowfully on the ground, and sighed gently to himself, "Alas! Who would dare accompany?"

"My poor good Sintram," said the Chaplain, in a tone of the softest kindness, "I understand you well, but the time has not yet come. The powers of evil will again raise up their wrathful heads within you, and Verena must check both her own and your longing desires, until all is pure in your spirit, as in hers. Comfort yourself with the thought that God looks mercifully upon you, and that the joy so earnestly sought for will come – if not here, most assuredly beyond the grave."

But Weigand, as though awaking out of a trance, rose mightily from his seat, and said, "Do you please to come forth with me, Reverend Chaplain? Before the sun appears in the heavens, we could reach the convent-gates, and I should not be far from Heaven."

In vain, the Chaplain and Rolf reminded him of his weakness. He smiled, and said that there could be no words about it; and he girded himself, and tuned the lute, which he had asked leave to take with him. His decided manner overcame all opposition, almost without words.

The Chaplain had already prepared himself for the journey, when Weigand looked with much emotion at Sintram, who, oppressed with a strange weariness, had sunk, half-asleep, on a couch, and said, "Wait a moment. I know that he wants me to give him a soft lullaby."

The pleased smile of the youth seemed to say, 'Yes', and Weigand, touching the strings with a light hand, sang these words:

Sleep peacefully, dear boy;
Thy mother sends the song
That whispers round thy couch,
To lull thee all night long.
In silence and afar
For thee she ever prays,
And longs once more in fondness
Upon thy face to gaze.

And when thy waking cometh,
Then in thy every deed,
In all that may betide thee,
Unto her words give heed.
Oh, listen for her voice,
If it be yea or nay;
And though temptation meet thee,
Thou shalt not miss the way.

If thou canst listen rightly,
And nobly onward go,
Then pure and gentle breezes
Around thy cheek shall blow.
Then on thy peaceful journey
Her blessing thou shalt feel,
And though from thee divided,
Her presence o'er thee steal.

O safest, sweetest comfort!
O blest and living light!
That, strong in Heaven's power,
All terrors put to flight!

Rest quietly, sweet child,
  And may the gentle numbers
Thy mother sends to thee
  Waft peace unto thy slumbers.

Sintram fell into a deep sleep, smiling, and breathing softly. Rolf and the Castellan remained by his bed, while the two travellers pursued their way in the quiet starlight.

CHAPTER XXII

The Bells for the Departed

THE dawn had almost appeared, when Rolf, who had been asleep, was awakened by low singing. As he looked round, he perceived, with surprise, that the sounds came from the lips of the Castellan, who said, as if in explanation, "So does Sir Weigand sing at the convent-gates, and they are kindly opened to him." Upon which, old Rolf fell asleep again, uncertain whether what had passed had been a dream or a reality.

After a while, the bright sunshine awoke Rolf again. When he rose up, he saw the countenance of the Castellan wonderfully illuminated by the red morning rays; and altogether those features, once so fearful, were shining with a soft, nay almost childlike, mildness. The mysterious man seemed to be listening to the motionless air, as if he were hearing a most pleasant discourse or lofty music; and as Rolf was about to speak, he made him a sign of entreaty to remain quiet, and continued in his eager listening attitude.

At length he sank slowly and contentedly back in his

seat, whispering, "God be praised! She has granted his last prayer. He will be laid in the burial-ground of the convent, and now he has forgiven me in the depths of his heart. I can assure you that he finds a peaceful end."

Rolf did not dare ask a question, or awake his lord. He felt as if one already departed had spoken to him.

The Castellan remained motionless for a long while, always smiling brightly. At last, he rose a little, again listened, and said, "It is over. The sound of the bells is very sweet. We have overcome. Oh, how soft and easy does the good God make it for us!" And so it came to pass; he stretched himself back, as if weary, and his soul was freed from his careworn body.

Rolf now gently awoke his young knight, and pointed to the smiling dead, and Sintram smiled too; he and his good esquire fell on their knees, and prayed to God for the departed spirit. Then they rose up and bore the cold body to the vaulted hall, and watched over it, with holy candles, until the return of the Chaplain. That the pilgrim would not come back again, they very well knew.

Accordingly, towards midday, the Chaplain returned alone. He could scarcely do more than confirm what was already known to them. He only added a comforting and hopeful greeting from Sintram's mother to her son, and told them that the blissful Weigand had fallen asleep like a tired child, whilst Verena, with calm tenderness, held a crucifix before him.

"And in eternal peace our penance end!" sang Sintram, gently to himself, and they prepared a last resting place for the now peaceful Castellan, and laid him therein with all the due solemn rites.

Soon afterwards, the Chaplain was obliged to depart; but when bidding Sintram farewell, he again said kindly to him, "Your dear mother assuredly knows how gentle and calm and good you are now!"

CHAPTER XXIII

The Customs of Yuletide

IN the castle of Sir Biorn of the Fiery Eyes, Christmas Eve had not passed so brightly and happily; but there too, all had visibly gone according to God's will.

Folko, at the entreaty of the Lord of the Castle, had allowed Gabrielle to support him into the hall; and the three now sat at the round stone table, where a sumptuous meal was laid. On either side there were long tables, at which sat the retainers of both knights in full armour, according to the custom of the north. Torches and lamps lit the lofty hall with an almost dazzling brightness.

Midnight had now begun its solemn reign, and Gabrielle softly reminded her wounded knight to withdraw. Biorn heard her, and said, "You are right, fair lady. Our knight needs rest. Only, let us first keep up one more old and honourable custom." And, at his sign, four attendants brought in, with pomp, a great boar's head, which looked as if had been cut out of solid gold, and placed it in the middle of the stone table. Biorn's retainers rose with reverence, and took off their helmets. Biorn himself did the same.

"What is meant by this?" Folko asked very gravely.

"This is what your forefathers and mine have done on every Yule feast," answered Biorn. "We are going to make vows on the boar's head, and then pass the goblet round to their fulfilment."

"We no longer keep what our ancestors called the Yule feast," said Folko. "We are good Christians, and we keep holy Christmastide."

"I hold my ancestors too dear to forget their knightly customs," answered Biorn. "Those who think otherwise may act according to their wisdom, but that shall not hinder me. I swear by the golden boar's head –" And he stretched out his hand, to lay it solemnly upon it.

However, Folko called out, "In the name of our holy Saviour, cease. Where I am, and still have breath and will, none shall celebrate the rites of the wild heathens undisturbed."

Biorn of the Fiery Eyes glared angrily at him. The men of the two Barons separated from each other, with a hollow sound of rattling armour, and ranged themselves in two bodies on either side of the hall, each behind its leader. Already, here and there, helmets were fastened and visors closed.

"Consider what you are doing," said Biorn. "I was about to vow an eternal union with the house of Montfaucon, nay, even to bind myself, to do it grateful homage. But if you disturb me in the customs, which have come to me from my forefathers, look to your safety and the safety of all that is dear to you. My wrath no longer knows any bounds."

Folko made a sign to the pale Gabrielle to retire behind his followers, saying to her, "Be of good cheer, my noble wife. Weaker Christians have braved, for the sake of God and of His holy Church, greater dangers than now seem to threaten us. Believe me, the Lord of Montfaucon is not so easily ensnared."

Somewhat comforted by Folko's fearless smile, Gabrielle obeyed, but his smile inflamed the fury of Biorn even more. Again, he stretched out his hand towards the boar's head, as if about to make some dreadful vow, when Folko snatched a gauntlet from Biorn's table, with which he, with his unwounded left arm, struck so powerful a blow on the gilt idol that it fell crashing to the ground, smashed to pieces.

Biorn and his followers stood as if turned to stone. However, swords were soon grasped by armed hands, shields were taken down from the walls, and an angry threatening murmur sounded through the hall.

At a sign from Folko, a battleaxe was brought to him by one of his faithful retainers. He swung it high in air with his powerful left hand, and stood, looking like an avenging angel, as he spoke, with awful calmness, these words through the tumult, "What do you seek, deluded Northman? What would you do, sinful lord? You have indeed become heathens, and I hope to show you, by my readiness for battle, that it is not in my right arm alone that God has put strength for victory. Nevertheless, if you can yet hear, listen to my words.

"Biorn, on this same accursed, and now, by God's help, fragmented boar's head, you did lay your hand when you did swear to sacrifice any inhabitants of the German towns that should fall into your power. And Gotthard Lenz came, and Rudlieb came, driven on these shores by the storm. What did you then do, savage Biorn? What did you do at his bidding, you who were keeping the Yule feast with him? Try your fortune on me. The Lord will be with me, as He was with those holy men. To arms, and –" he turned to his warriors "– let our battle-cry be Gotthard and Rudlieb!"

Then Biorn let drop his drawn sword, then his followers paused, and none among the Norwegians dared lift his eyes from the ground. By degrees, they began to disappear from the hall, and at last, Biorn stood quite alone opposite the Baron and his followers.

Biorn seemed hardly aware that he had been deserted as he fell on his knees, stretched out his shining sword, pointed to the broken boar's head, and said, "Do with me as you have done with that. I deserve no better. I ask but one favour, only one. Do not disgrace me, noble Baron, by seeking shelter in another castle of Norway."

"I fear you not," answered Folko, after some thought, "and, as far as may be, I freely forgive you." Then he drew the Sign of the Cross over the wild form of Biorn, and left the hall with Gabrielle. The retainers of the house of Montfaucon followed him, proudly and silently.

The hard spirit of the fierce Lord of the Castle was now quite broken, and he watched, with increased humility, every look of Folko and Gabrielle. However, they withdrew more and more into the happy solitude of their own apartments, where they enjoyed, in the midst of the sharp winter, a bright springtide of happiness.

The wounded condition of Folko did not hinder the evening delights of songs and music and poetry. Indeed, it added a new charm to them when the tall handsome knight leant on the arm of his delicate lady, and, in this manner, they walked slowly through the torch-lit halls, scattering their kindly greetings like flowers among the crowds of men and women.

CHAPTER XXIV

The Passage into Darkness

ALL this time, little or nothing was heard of poor Sintram. The last wild outbreak of his father had increased the terror with which Gabrielle remembered the self-accusations of the youth; and the more resolutely that Folko kept his silence, the more did she foretell of some dreadful mystery.

Indeed, a secret shudder came over Folko whenever he thought of the pale dark-haired youth. Sintram's repentance had bordered on settled despair; no one even knew what he was doing in that fortress of evil-report on the Rocks of the Moon. Strange rumours were brought by the retainers who had fled from it, that the evil spirit had obtained complete power over Sintram, that no man could stay with him and that the fidelity of the dark mysterious Castellan had cost him his life. Folko could hardly drive away the fearful suspicion that the lonely young knight had become a wicked magician.

And perhaps evil spirits did flit about the banished Sintram, but it was without his calling them up. In his dreams, he often saw the wicked goddess Aphrodite, in her golden chariot drawn by doves, pass over the battlements of the stone fortress, and heard her say to him mockingly, "Foolish Sintram, foolish Sintram! Had you but obeyed the Little Master! You would now be in Helen's arms, and the Rocks of the Moon would be called the Rocks of Love and the stone fortress would be the Garden of Roses.

"You would have lost your pale face and dark hair – for you are only enchanted, dear youth – and your eyes would have beamed more softly, and your cheeks bloomed more freshly, and your hair would have been more golden than was that of Paris when men wondered at his beauty. Oh, how Helen would have loved you!"

Then Aphrodite showed him in a mirror, how, as a marvellously beautiful knight, he knelt before Gabrielle, who sank into his arms, blushing as the morning. When he awoke from such dreams, he would eagerly seize the sword and scarf given him by his lady – as a shipwrecked man seizes the plank that will save him – and while the hot tears fell on them, he would murmur to himself, "There was, indeed, one hour in my sad life when I was worthy and happy."

Once he sprang up at midnight, after one of these dreams, but this time with more thrilling horror; for it had seemed to him that the features of the goddess Aphrodite had changed towards the end of her speech, as she looked down upon him with marvellous scorn, and she appeared to him as the hideous Little Master.

The youth had no better means of calming his distracted mind than to throw the sword and scarf of

Gabrielle over his shoulders, and to hasten outward under the solemn starry canopy of the wintry sky. He walked in deep thought, backwards and forwards under the leafless oaks and the snow-laden firs that grew on the high ramparts.

Then he heard a sorrowful cry of distress sound from the moat; it was as if someone was attempting to sing, but was stopped by inward grief. Sintram exclaimed, "Who's there?" and all was still.

When he was silent, and again began his walk, the frightful groans and moans were heard afresh, as if they came from a dying person.

Sintram overcame the horror that seemed to hold him back, and began, in silence, to climb down into the deep dry moat, which was cut into the rock. He was soon so low down that he could no longer see the stars shining. Beneath him moved a shrouded form and, sliding with involuntary haste down the steep descent, he stood near the groaning figure.

It ceased its lamentations, and began to laugh like a maniac from beneath its long folded female garments. "Oh ho, my comrade! Oh ho, my comrade! Were you going a little too fast? Well, well, it is all right. And see now, you stand no higher than I do, my pious valiant youth! Take it patiently. Take it patiently!"

"What do you want with me? Why do you laugh? Why do you weep?" asked Sintram impatiently.

"I might ask you the same questions," answered the dark figure, "and you would be less able to answer me than I to answer you. Why do you laugh? Why do you weep? Poor creature! But I will show you a remarkable thing in your fortress, of which you know nothing." And the shrouded figure began to scratch and scrape at the stones until a little iron door opened, and showed a long passage, which led into the deep darkness.

"Will you come with me?" whispered the strange being. "It is the shortest way to your father's castle. In half-an-hour, we shall come out of this passage, and we shall be in your beauteous lady's apartment. King Menelaus shall lie in a magic sleep — leave that to me — and then you will take the slight delicate form in your arms, and bring her to the Rocks of the Moon. You will win back all that seemed lost by your former wavering."

Sintram visibly trembled, fearfully shaken by the fever of passion and the stings of conscience. But, at last, pressing the sword and scarf to his heart, he cried out, "Oh, that fairest, most glorious hour of my life! If I lose all other joys, I will hold fast that brightest hour!"

"A bright, glorious hour!" said the figure from under its veil, like an evil echo. "Do you know whom you then conquered? A good old friend, who only showed himself to give you the glory of overcoming him. Will you convince yourself? Will you look?"

The dark garments of the little figure flew open, and the dwarf warrior in strange armour, the gold horns on his helmet and the curved spear in his hand, the very same whom Sintram thought he had slain on Niflung's Heath, now stood before him and laughed.

"You see, my youth, everything in the wide world is but dreams and froth, which is why you must hold fast to the dream which delights you, and sip up the froth which refreshes you! Hasten to that underground passage, it leads up to your angel Helen. Or would you first know your friend yet better?" And the dwarf warrior's visor opened and the hateful face of the Little Master glared upon the knight.

As if in a dream, Sintram asked, "Are you also that wicked goddess Aphrodite?"

"Something like her," answered the Little Master, laughing, "or rather she is something like me. And if you will only get disenchanted, and recover the beauty of Prince Paris – then, Prince Paris," and his voice changed to an alluring song, "I shall be fair like you!"

At this moment, the good Rolf appeared above on the rampart; a consecrated taper in his lantern shone down into the moat, as he sought for the missing young knight. "In God's name, Sir Sintram," he called out, "what has the spectre of whom you slew on Niflung's Heath, and whom I never could bury, to do with you?"

"See you well? Hear you well?" whispered the Little Master, and drew back into the darkness of the underground passage. "The wise man up there knows me well. There was nothing in your heroic feat. Come. Take the joys of life while you can."

However, Sintram sprang back, with a strong effort, into the circle of light made by the shining of the taper from above, and cried out, "Depart from me, unquiet spirit! I know well that I bear a name on me in which you can have no part."

In fear and rage, the Little Master rushed into the

passage, and, yelling, shut the iron door behind him. It seemed as if he could still be heard groaning and roaring.

Sintram climbed up the wall of the moat, and made a sign to his foster-father not to speak to him. He only said, "One of my best joys, yes, the very best, has been taken from me. But, by God's help, I am not yet lost."

In the earliest light of the following morning, he and Rolf stopped up the entrance to the perilous passage with huge blocks of stone.

CHAPTER XXV

The Montfaucons Take Their Leave

THE long northern winter was at last at an end. The fresh green leaves rustled merrily in the woods, patches of soft moss twinkled amongst the rocks, the valleys grew green, the brooks sparkled, the snow melted from all but the highest mountaintops, and the bark[11], which was ready to carry away Folko and Gabrielle, danced on the sunny waves of the sea.

One morning, the Baron, now quite recovered, and strong and fresh as though his health had sustained no injury, stood on the shore with his fair lady. Full of glee at the prospect of returning to their home, the noble pair looked on, well pleased, as their attendants busily laded the ship.

Then, in the midst of a confused sound of many voices, one of the attendants said, "But what has appeared to me the most fearful and strange thing in this northern land is the stone fortress on the Rocks of the Moon. Although, I have never been inside it, I used to see it on our hunts, towering above the tall fir-trees, and a tightness would come over my breast, as if something unearthly were dwelling in it.

"And a few weeks ago, when the snow was still lying hard in the valleys, I came unawares quite close upon the strange building. The young Knight Sintram was walking alone on the ramparts as twilight came on, like the spirit of a departed knight, and he drew from the lute, which he carried, such soft melancholy tones, and he sighed so deeply and sorrowfully ..."

The noise of the crowd drowned out the voice of the speaker, and as he had also just then reached the ship, Folko and Gabrielle were unable to hear the rest of his speech, but the fair lady looked on her knight, eyes dimmed with tears, and sighed. "Does the Rocks of the Moon not lie behind those mountains? The unhappy Sintram makes me sad at heart."

"I understand you, sweet gracious lady, and the pure compassion of your heart," replied Folko, instantly ordering his swift-footed steed to be brought. He placed his noble lady under the charge of his retainers, and leaping into the saddle, he hastened, followed by the grateful smiles of Gabrielle, along the valley towards the stone fortress.

Sintram was seated near the drawbridge, touching the strings of his lute, and shedding some tears on the golden chords, almost as Montfaucon's esquire had described him. Suddenly a cloudy shadow passed over him, and he looked up, expecting to see a flight of cranes in the air, but the sky was clear and blue.

While the young Knight was still wondering, a long

bright spear fell at his feet from a battlement of the armoury turret. "Take it up. Make good use of it! Your foe is near at hand! Near also is the downfall of your dearest happiness," he heard distinctly whispered in his ear, and it seemed to him that he saw the shadow of the Little Master glide close by him to a neighbouring cleft in the rock.

At the same time, a tall gigantic haggard figure passed along the valley, alike the departed pilgrim in some measure, only much larger, and he raised his long bony arm, fearfully threatening, before disappearing into an ancient tomb.

In the next instant, Sir Folko of Montfaucon came up the Rocks of the Moon as swiftly as the wind, and he must have seen something of those strange apparitions, for as he stopped close behind Sintram, he looked rather pale, and asked, low and earnestly, "Sir Knight, who are those two with whom you were just now conversing?"

"The good God knows," answered Sintram. "I know them not."

"If the good God does but know!" cried Montfaucon. "But I fear that He knows very little of you or your deeds."

"You speak strangely harsh words," said Sintram. "Yet, ever since that evening of misery – even long before – I must bear with all that comes from you. Dear Sir, you may believe me, I know not those fearful companions. I call them not, and I know not what terrible curse binds them to my footsteps.

"The merciful God, as I would hope, is mindful of me all the while – as a faithful shepherd does not forget even the worst and most widely-straying of his flock, but calls after it with an anxious voice in the gloomy wilderness."

The anger of the Baron quite melted, and two bright tears stood in his eyes as he said, "No, assuredly, God has not forgotten you. Only do not forget your gracious God. I did not come to rebuke you. I came to bless you in Gabrielle's name and in my own. May the Lord preserve you, guide you, and lift you up!

"And, Sintram, on the far-off shores of Normandy, I shall bear you in mind, and I shall hear how you struggled against the curse which weighs down your unhappy life. And if you ever shake it off, and stand as a noble conqueror over Sin and Death, then you shall receive from me a token of love and reward, more precious then either you or I can understand at this moment."

The words flowed prophetically from the Baron's lips; he himself was only half-conscious of what he said. With a kind salutation, he turned his noble steed, and again flew down the valley towards the seashore.

"Fool! Fool! Thrice a fool!" whispered the angry voice of the Little Master in Sintram's ear. However, old Rolf was singing his morning hymn in clear tones within the castle, and the last lines were these:

> *Whom worldlings scorn,*
> *Who lives forlorn,*
> *   On God's own word doth rest;*
>
> *With heavenly light*
> *His path is bright,*
> *   His lot among the blest.*

Then a holy joy took possession of Sintram's heart, and he looked around him more gladly than in the hour when Gabrielle gave him the scarf and sword, and Folko dubbed him 'Knight'.

CHAPTER XXVI

The True Nature of Biorn

BIORN of the Fiery Eye still sat, gloomy and speechless, in his castle as the Baron and his lovely lady sailed across the broad sea with favouring gales of spring, the coast of Normandy already in sight, above the waves. He had taken no leave of his guests. There was more proud fear of Montfaucon than reverential love for him in his soul, especially since the incident with the boar's head, and the thought was bitter to his haughty spirit.

That the great Baron, the flower and glory of their whole race, had come in peace to visit him and now departed in stern reproachful displeasure was yet another bitter thought. Biorn had it constantly at the forefront of his mind, and the remembrance of how all had come to pass never failed to bring fresh pangs. So too, did the remembrance of how all might have gone otherwise; and he was always fancying that he could hear the songs in which later generations would recount this voyage of the great Folko, and the worthlessness of the savage Biorn.

At length, full of fierce anger, he cast away the

fetters of his troubled spirit. He burst out of the castle with all his horsemen, and began to carry on a warfare more fearful and more lawless than any in which he had previously engaged.

Sintram heard the sound of his father's war-horn and, committing the stone fortress to old Rolf, he sprang forth, ready armed for the combat. However, the flames of the cottages and farms on the mountains rose up before him, and showed him – written in characters of fire – what kind of war his father was waging.

Yet he went on, towards the spot where the army was mustered, but only to offer his mediation, affirming that he would not lay his hand on his sword in support of such an abhorrent service, even if the stone fortress, and his father's castle, should fall before the vengeance of their enemies.

Mad with fury, Biorn hurled the spear that he held in his hand against his son. The deadly weapon whizzed past Sintram and he remained standing, with his visor raised. He did not move one limb in his defence, when he said, "Father, do what you will, but I will not join you in your godless warfare."

Biorn of the Fiery Eyes laughed scornfully, "It seems I am always to have a spy over me. My son succeeds the dainty French Knight!" Nevertheless, he came to himself, accepted Sintram's mediation, made amends for the injuries he had done, and returned gloomily to his castle. Sintram went back to the Rocks of the Moon.

After that time, such occurrences were frequent. It went so far that Sintram came to be looked upon as the protector of all those whom his father pursued with relentless fury. Nevertheless, his own wildness would sometimes carry the young knight away to accompany his fierce father in his fearful deeds.

Then Biorn would laugh with horrible pleasure, and say, "See there, my son, how the flames we have lighted blaze up from the villages, as the blood spouts up from the wounds our swords have made! It is plain to me, however much you may pretend to the contrary, that you are, and will ever remain, my true and beloved heir!"

After such fearfully lapses, Sintram could find no comfort but in hastening to the Chaplain of Drontheim, and confessing to him all his misery and sins.

After due penance and repentance, the Chaplain would freely absolve him and again raise the broken-hearted youth back up. Though often he would say, "Oh, how nearly had you reached your last trial, and gained the victory, and looked on Aphrodite's countenance, and atoned for all! Now you have thrown yourself back years. Think, my son, on the shortness of man's life. If you are always falling back anew, how will you ever gain the summit on this side of the grave?"

CHAPTER XXVII

A Battle of Wills

YEARS came and went. Biorn's hair was white as snow, and the youth Sintram had reached middle age. Old Rolf was now scarcely able to leave the stone fortress, and sometimes he said, "I feel it a burden that my life should yet be prolonged, but also there is much comfort in it, for I still think the good God has some great happiness in store for me here below. And it must be something in which you are concerned, my beloved Sir Sintram, for what else in the whole world could rejoice me?" However, all remained as it was, and the fearful dreams Sintram experienced each year at Christmastime increased, rather than diminished, in horror.

Again, the holy season was drawing near, and the mind of the sorely afflicted knight was more troubled than ever before. Sometimes, if he had been reckoning up the nights until it should come, a cold sweat would stand on his forehead, while he said, "Mark my words, dear old foster-father, something most awfully decisive lies before me this time."

One evening, he felt an overwhelming anxiety about his father. It seemed to him that the Prince of Darkness was going up to Biorn's castle. In vain, Rolf reminded Sintram that the snow laid deep in the valleys; in vain, he suggested that, during the night, his frightful dreams might overtake him in the lonely mountains.

"Nothing can be worse to me than remaining here would be," replied Sintram, and he took his horse from the stable and rode forth in the gathering darkness. The noble steed slipped and stumbled and fell in the trackless way, but his rider always raised him up, and urged him more swiftly and eagerly towards the object which he longed and yet dreaded to reach.

Nevertheless, Sintram might never have arrived at his father's castle had not his faithful hound, Skovmark, kept pace him. The dog sought out the lost track for his beloved master, and invited him into it with joyous barks. By his howls, he warned Sintram against precipices and treacherous ice under the snow.

It was in this manner that they arrived, about midnight, at Biorn's castle. The windows of the hall shone with a brilliant light, as though some great feast were kept there, and confused sounds, as of singing, met their ears. Sintram hastily gave his horse to some retainers in the courtyard, and ran up the steps, whilst Skovmark stayed by the well-known horse.

A good esquire came towards Sintram within the castle and said, "God be praised, my dear master, that you have come, for surely nothing good is going on above. Yet take heed to yourself also, and do not be deluded. Your father has a guest with him – and, as I think – a hateful one."

Sintram shuddered as he threw open the doors. A little man, in the dress of a miner, was sitting with his back towards him. The armour had been, for some time past, ranged round the stone table so that only two places were left empty. Biorn of the Fiery Eyes had taken the seat opposite the door, and the dazzling light of the torches fell upon his features with so red a flare that he perfectly enacted that fearful surname.

"Father, whom have you here with you?" cried Sintram, and his suspicions rose to certainty as the miner turned round, and the detestable face of the Little Master grinned from under his dark hood.

"Yes, just see, my fair son," said the wild Biorn, "you have not been here for a long while, and so tonight, this jolly comrade has paid me a visit, and your place has been taken. But throw one of the suits of armour out of the way, and claim a seat for yourself – then come and drink with us, and be merry."

"Yes, do so, Sir Sintram," said the Little Master, with a laugh. "Nothing worse could come of it than that the broken pieces of armour might clatter somewhat strangely together or, at most, that the disturbed spirit of him to whom the suit belonged might look over your shoulder. But he would not drink up any of our wine. Ghosts have nothing to do with that. So now fall to!"

Biorn joined in the laughter of the hideous stranger with wild mirth; and while Sintram was mustering up his whole strength not to lose his senses at such terrible words, and was fixing a calm steady look on the Little

Master's face, the old man cried out, "Why do you look at him so? Does it seem as though you saw yourself in a mirror? Now that you are together, I do not see it so much. But, a while ago, I thought that you were enough alike as to be mistaken for each other."

"God forbid!" said Sintram, walking up close to the fearful apparition. "I command you, detestable stranger, to depart from this castle, by right of my authority as my father's heir, as a consecrated knight and as a spirit!"

Biorn seemed as if he wished to oppose himself to this command with all his savage might, however, the Little Master muttered, "You are not by any means the master in this house, pious knight. You have never lighted a fire on this hearth."

Then Sintram drew the sword that Gabrielle had given him, held the cross of the hilt before the eyes of his evil guest, and said, calmly, but with a powerful voice, "Worship or fly!" And he fled, the frightful stranger. He fled with such lightning speed, that those present could scarcely see whether he had sprung through the window or the door.

However, in going, he overthrew some of the armour, the tapers went out, and it seemed that the pale blue flame, which lit up the whole in a marvellous manner, gave fulfilment to the Little Master's former words, and that the spirits of those to whom the armour had belonged were leaning over the table, grinning fearfully.

Both the father and the son were filled with horror, but each chose an opposite way to save himself. Biorn wished to have his hateful guest back again, and the

147

power of his will was seen when the Little Master's step resounded anew on the stairs and his brown shrivelled hand shook the lock of the door. On the other hand, Sintram never ceased to say within himself, "We are lost, if he comes back! We are lost to all eternity, if he comes back!" And he fell on his knees, and prayed fervently from his troubled heart to the Father, Son, and Holy Ghost.

In response, the Little Master left the door. Again, Biorn willed him to return, and again Sintram's prayers drove him away. So went on this strife of wills throughout the long night; and howling whirlwinds raged the while around the castle, until all the household thought the end of the world was come.

At length, the dawn of morning appeared through the windows of the hall – the fury of the storm was lulled. Biorn sank back, powerless in slumber, on his seat. Peace and hope came to the inmates of the castle, and Sintram, pale and exhausted, went out to breathe the dewy air of the mild winter's morning before the castle-gates.

CHAPTER XXVIII

The Preparations for the Trial

THE faithful Skovmark followed his master, caressing him; and when Sintram fell asleep on a stone seat in the wall, he lay at his feet, keeping watchful guard. Suddenly he pricked up his ears, looked round with delight, and bounded joyfully down the mountain. Just afterwards, the Chaplain of Drontheim appeared amongst the rocks, and the good beast went up to him, as if to greet him, and then again ran back to the Knight to announce the welcome visitor.

Sintram opened his eyes, as a child whose Christmas gifts have been placed at his bedside, for the Chaplain smiled at him as he had never yet seen him smile, and there was in it a token of victory and blessing, or at least of the near approach of both.

"You did much yesterday, very much," said the holy priest; and his hands were joined, and his eyes full of bright tears. "I praise God for you, my noble knight. Verena knows all, and she too praises God for you. Indeed, I do now dare to hope that the time will soon come when you may appear before her.

"But Sintram, dear Sintram, there is need of haste. For the old man above requires speedy air, and you have still a heavy – as I hope, the last – yet a most heavy trial to undergo for His sake. Arm yourself, my knight; arm yourself even with bodily weapons. In truth, this time only spiritual armour is needed, but it always befits a knight, as well as a monk, to wear the entire solemn garb of his station in decisive moments.

"If it so pleases you, we will go directly to Drontheim together. You must return there tonight. Such is a part of the hidden decree, which has been dimly unfolded to Verena's foresight. There is much that is wild and distracting here, and today you have great need of calm preparation."

With humble joy, Sintram bowed his assent, and called for his horse and a suit of armour. "Only," he added, "do not let any of that armour, which was overthrown in the hall last night, be brought!"

His orders were quickly obeyed. The arms which were fetched, adorned with fine engraved work, the simple helmet, formed rather like that of an esquire than a knight, the lance of almost gigantic size, which belonged to the suit – on all these the Chaplain gazed in deep thought and with melancholy emotion.

At last, when Sintram, with the help of his esquires, was well nigh equipped, the holy priest spoke, "Wonderful providence of God! See, dear Sintram, this armour and spear were formerly those of Sir Weigand the Slender, and with them he did many mighty deeds.

"When he was tended by your mother in the castle, and when your father still showed himself kind towards him, he asked, as a favour, that his armour and his lance should be allowed to hang in Biorn's armoury. Weigand himself, as you well know, intended to build a cloister and to live there as a monk, therefore he had no further need of it. He also put his old esquire's helmet with it, instead of another, because he was wearing that one when he first saw the fair Verena's angelic face.

"How wondrously does it now come to pass, that these very arms, which have so long been laid aside, should be brought to you for the decisive hour of your life! To me, as far as my short-sighted human wisdom can tell, it truly seems a very solemn token, but one full of high and glorious promise."

Sintram now stood in complete array, composed and stately, and, from his tall slender figure, he might have been taken for a youth, had not the deep lines of care, which furrowed his countenance, shown him to be advanced in years.

"Who has placed boughs on the head of my warhorse?" asked Sintram of the esquires, with displeasure. "I am not a conqueror, nor a wedding-guest. And besides, there are no boughs now but those red and yellow crackling oak-leaves, dull and dead like the season itself."

"Sir Knight, I know not myself," answered an esquire, "but it seemed to me that it must be so."

"Let it be," said the Chaplain. "I feel that this also comes as a token full of meaning from the right source."

Then the knight threw himself into his saddle, the priest went beside him, and they both rode slowly and silently towards Drontheim. The faithful dog followed his master.

When the lofty castle of Drontheim appeared in sight, a gentle smile spread itself over Sintram's countenance, like sunshine over a wintry valley. "God has done great things for me," said he. "I once rushed from here, a fearfully wild boy. I now come back a penitent man. I trust that it will yet go well with my poor troubled life."

The Chaplain assented kindly, and soon afterwards, the travellers passed under the echoing vaulted gateway into the castle-yard.

At a sign from the Chaplain, the retainers approached with respectful haste, and took charge of the horse; then he and Sintram went through long winding passages and up many steps to the remote chamber, which the Chaplain had chosen for himself, far away from the noise of men, and near to the clouds and the stars. There the two passed a quiet day in devout prayer, and earnest reading of Holy Scripture.

When the evening began to close in, the Chaplain arose and said, "And now, my knight, get your horse ready, and mount and ride back again to your father's castle. A toilsome way lies before you, and I dare not go with you. But I can, and will, call upon the Lord for you all through the long fearful night. Oh, beloved instrument of the Most High, you will yet not be lost!"

Thrilling with strange forebodings, but nevertheless strong and vigorous in spirit, Sintram did according to the holy man's desire. The sun set as the knight approached a long valley, strangely shut in by rocks, through which lay the road to his father's castle.

CHAPTER XXIX

The Peal of the Passing Bell

BEFORE entering the rocky pass, the knight, with a prayer and thanksgiving, looked back once more at the Castle of Drontheim. There it was, so vast, so quiet, and so peaceful; the bright windows of the Chaplain's high chamber yet lit up by the last gleam of the sun, which had already disappeared.

In front of Sintram was the gloomy valley, as if his grave. Then there came towards him someone riding on a small horse; and Skovmark, who had gone up to the stranger as if to find out who he was, now ran back with his tail between his legs and his ears put back, howling and whining, and crept, terrified, under his master's warhorse.

Even the noble steed appeared to have forgotten his once so fearless and warlike ardour. He trembled violently, and when the knight would have turned him towards the stranger, he reared and snorted and plunged, and began to throw himself backwards. It was only with difficulty that Sintram's strength and horsemanship got the better of him; and he was all white with foam when Sintram came up to the unknown traveller.

"You have cowardly beasts with you," said the latter, in a low smothered voice.

In the ever-increasing darkness, Sintram was unable to distinguish correctly what kind of being he saw before him. Only a very pallid face, which at first he had thought was covered with freshly fallen snow, met his eyes from amidst the long hanging garments. It seemed that the stranger carried a small box wrapped up; his little horse, as if wearied out, bent his head down towards the ground, whereby a bell, which hung from the wretched torn bridle under his neck, was made to give a strange sound.

After a short silence, Sintram replied, "Noble steeds avoid those of a worse race, because they are ashamed of them, and the boldest dogs are attacked by a secret terror at the sight of forms to which they are not accustomed. I have no cowardly beasts with me."

"Good, Sir Knight, then ride with me through the valley."

"I am going through the valley, but I want no companions."

"But perhaps I want one. Do you not see that I am unarmed? And at this season, at this hour, there are frightful unearthly beasts about."

Just then, as though to confirm the awful words of the stranger, a thing swung itself down from one of the nearest trees, covered with hoar-frost – no-one could say if it were a snake or a lizard – it curled and twisted itself, and appeared about to slide down upon the knight or his companion.

Sintram levelled his spear, and pierced the creature through. However, with the most hideous contortions, it fixed itself firmly on the spearhead; and, in vain, did the knight endeavour to rub it off against the rocks or the trees. Then he let his spear rest upon his right shoulder, with the point behind him, so that the horrible beast no longer met his sight; and he said, with good courage, to the stranger, "It does seem, indeed, that I could help you, and I am not forbidden to have an unknown stranger in my company. So, let us push on bravely into the valley!"

"Help!" resounded the solemn answer. "Not help. I perhaps may help you. But God have mercy upon you if the time should ever come when I could no longer help you. Then you would be lost, and I should become very frightful to you. But we will go through the valley. I have your knightly word on it. Come!"

They rode forward; Sintram's horse still showing signs of fear, the faithful dog still whining, but both obedient to their master's will. The knight was calm and steadfast.

The snow had slipped down from the smooth rocks and, by the light of the rising moon, various strange twisted shapes could be seen on their sides – some looking like snakes, and some like human faces. However, the shapes were only formed by the veins in the rock and the half-bare roots of trees, which had planted themselves in that desert place with capricious firmness.

High above, and at a great distance, the Castle of Drontheim, as if to take leave, appeared again through an opening in the rocks. The knight then looked keenly at his companion, and he almost felt as if Weigand the Slender were riding beside him. "In God's name," he cried, "are you not the shade of that departed knight who suffered and died for Verena?"

"I have not suffered, I have not died. But you suffer, and you die, poor mortals!" murmured the stranger. "I am not Weigand. I am that other, who was so like him, and whom you have also met before now in the wood."

Sintram strove to free himself from the terror that came over him at these words. He looked at his horse; it appeared to him entirely altered. In the uncertain moonlight, the dry many-coloured oak-leaves on its head were waving like the flames around a sacrifice.

He looked down again, to see after his faithful Skovmark. Fear had likewise most wondrously changed him. On the ground in the middle of the road were lying dead men's bones, and hideous lizards were crawling about; and, in defiance of the wintry season, poisonous mushrooms were growing up all around.

"Can this still be my horse on which I am riding?" said the knight to himself, in a low voice. "And can that trembling beast which runs at my side be my dog?"

Then someone called after him, in a yelling voice, "Stop! Stop! Take me also with you!"

Looking round, Sintram perceived a small frightful figure with horns, and a face partly like a wild boar and partly like a bear, walking along on its hind-legs, which were those of a horse; and in its hand was a strange hideous weapon, shaped like a hook or a sickle.

It was the being who had troubled him in his dreams; and – alas! – it was also the wretched Little Master himself, who, laughing wildly, stretched out a long claw towards the knight.

The bewildered Sintram murmured, "I must have fallen asleep, and now my dreams are coming over me!"

"You are awake," replied the rider of the little horse, "but you know me also in your dreams. For, behold! I am Death." And his garments fell from him, and there appeared a mouldering skeleton, its ghastly head crowned with serpents. That which he had kept hidden under his mantle was an hourglass with the sand almost run out. Death held it towards the knight in his fleshless hand. The bell at the neck of the little horse gave forth a solemn sound. It was a passing bell.

"Lord, into Your hands I commend my spirit!" prayed Sintram, and full of earnest devotion he rode after Death, who beckoned him on.

"He does not have you yet! He does not have you yet!" screamed the fearful fiend. "Give yourself up to me instead. In one instant – for swift are your thoughts and swift is my might – in one instant, you shall be in Normandy. Helen yet blooms in beauty as when she departed here, and this very night she would be yours." And, once again, he began his unholy praises of Gabrielle's loveliness, and Sintram's heart glowed like wildfire in his weak breast.

Death said nothing more, but raised the hourglass in his right hand yet higher and higher. And, as the sand now ran out more quickly, a soft light streamed from the glass over Sintram's countenance, and then it seemed to him as if eternity, in all its calm majesty, were rising before him, and a world of confusion dragging him back with a deadly grasp.

"I command you, wild form that follows me," he cried, "I command you, in the name of our Lord Jesus Christ, to cease from your seducing words, and to call yourself by that name by which you are recorded in Holy Writ!"

A name, more fearful than a thunderclap, burst despairingly from the lips of the Tempter, and he disappeared.

"He will return no more," said Death, in a kindly tone.

"And now I am become wholly yours, my stern companion?"

"Not yet, my Sintram. I shall not come to you until many years are past. But you must not forget me in the meantime."

"I will keep the thought of you steadily before my soul, you fearful yet wholesome monitor, you awful yet loving guide!"

"Oh! I can truly appear very gentle." And so it proved. His form became more softly defined in the increasing gleam of light that shone from the hourglass; the features, which had been awful in their sternness, wore a gentle smile; the crown of serpents became a bright palm-wreath. Instead of the horse, a white misty cloud appeared in the moonlight; and the bell gave forth sounds as of sweet lullabies. Sintram thought he could hear these words amidst them:

> *"The world and Satan are o'ercome,*
> *Before thee gleams eternal light,*
> *Warrior, who hast won the strife:*
> *Save from darkest shades of night*
> *Him before whose aged eyes*
> *All my terrors soon shall rise."*

The knight well knew that his father was meant; and he urged on his noble steed, which now obeyed his master willingly and gladly, and the faithful dog again ran beside him fearlessly.

Death had disappeared; but, in front of Sintram, there floated a bright morning cloud, which continued to be visible after the sun had risen, clear and warm in the bright winter sky.

CHAPTER XXX

The Passing of Biorn

"HE is dead! The horrors of that fearful stormy night have killed him!" said some of Biorn's retainers, who had not been able to bring him back to his senses since the morning of the day before. They had made a couch of wolf and bearskins for him in the Great Hall, in the midst of the armour, which still lay scattered around.

One of the esquires said with a low sigh, "May the Lord have mercy on his poor wild soul!"

Just then, the warder blew his horn from his tower, and a trooper came into the room with a look of surprise. "A knight is coming here," said he, "a wonderful knight. I could have taken him for our Lord Sintram, but a bright morning cloud floats so close before him, and throws over him such a clear light, that one could fancy red flowers showered down upon him. Besides, his horse has a wreath of red leaves on his head, which was never a custom of the son of our dead lord."

"Just such a one," replied another, "I wove for him yesterday. He was not pleased with it at first, but afterwards he let it remain."

"But why did you do that?"

"It seemed to me as if I heard a voice singing again and again in my ear, 'Victory! Victory! The noblest victory! The knight rides forth to victory!' And then I saw a branch of our oldest oak-tree stretched towards me, which had kept on almost all its red and yellow leaves in spite of the snow.

"So I did according to what I had heard sung, and I plucked some of the leaves, and wove a triumphal wreath for the noble warhorse. At the same time Skovmark – you know that the faithful beast had always a great dislike to Biorn, and therefore had gone to the stable with the horse – Skovmark jumped upon me, fawning, and seemed pleased, as if he wanted to thank me for my work. And such noble animals understand well about good omens." They heard the sound of Sintram's spurs on the stone steps, and Skovmark's joyous bark.

At that instant, the supposed corpse of old Biorn sat up, looked around with rolling staring eyes, and asked of the terrified retainers in a hollow voice, "Who comes there, you people? Who comes there? I know it is my son, but who comes with him? The answer to that bears the sword of decision in its mouth. For see, good people, Gotthard and Rudlieb have prayed much for me, yet if it the Little Master who comes with him, I am lost in spite of them."

"You are not lost, my beloved father!" Sintram's kind voice was heard to say, as he softly opened the door, and the bright red morning cloud floated in with him.

Biorn joined his hands, cast a look of thankfulness up to Heaven, and said, smiling, "Yes, praised be God! It is the right companion! It is sweet gentle death!" Then he made a sign to his son to approach, saying, "Come here, my deliverer. Come, blessed of the Lord, that I may relate to you all that has passed within me."

As Sintram now sat close by his father's couch, all who were in the room perceived a remarkable and striking change. For old Biorn, whose whole countenance – and not his eyes alone – had been accustomed to have a fiery aspect, was now quite pale, almost like white marble. While, on the other hand, the cheeks of the once deadly pale Sintram glowed with a bright bloom like that of early youth; the cause of which was the morning cloud, which still shone upon him and whose presence in the room was felt rather than seen, yet it produced a gentle thrill in every heart.

"See, my son," began the old man, softly and mildly, "I have lain for a long time in a deathlike sleep, and have known nothing of what was going on around me, but within – ah, within – I have known but too much! I thought that the eternal anguish would destroy my soul, and yet I felt, with much greater horror, that my soul was eternal, like that anguish. Beloved son, your cheeks that glowed so brightly are beginning to grow pale at my words. I refrain from more, but let me relate to you something more cheerful.

"Far away, I could see a bright lofty church, where Gotthard and Rudlieb Lenz were kneeling and praying for me. Gotthard had grown very old, and looked almost like one of our mountains covered with snow, on which the sun, in the lovely evening hours, is shining. Rudlieb was an elderly man, but very vigorous and very strong. And they both, with all their strength and vigour, were calling upon God to aid me, their enemy.

"Then I heard a voice, like that of an angel, saying, 'His son does the most for him! He must this night wrestle with death and with the fallen one! His victory will be victory, and his defeat will be defeat, for the old man and himself.' At that point, I awoke, and I knew that all depended upon whom you would bring with you. You have conquered. Next to God, the praise is to you!"

"Gotthard and Rudlieb have helped much," replied Sintram. "And, beloved father, so have the fervent prayers of the Chaplain of Drontheim. I felt, when struggling with temptation and deadly fear, how the heavenly breath of holy men floated round me and aided me."

"I am most willing to believe that, my noble son, and everything you say to me," answered the old man. At the same moment, the Chaplain also came in, and Biorn stretched out his hand towards him with a smile of peace and joy. Now, all seemed to be surrounded with a bright circle of unity and blessedness. "But see," said old Biorn, "how the faithful Skovmark jumps upon me now, and tries to caress me. It is not long since he used always to howl with terror when he saw me."

"My dear lord," said the Chaplain, "there is a spirit dwelling in good beasts, though dreamy and unconscious."

As the day wore on, the stillness in the hall increased. The last hour of the aged Knight was drawing near, but he met it calmly and fearlessly.

The Chaplain and Sintram prayed beside his couch. The retainers knelt devoutly around. At length, the dying man said, "Is that the prayer-bell in Verena's cloister?"

Sintram's looks said, 'Yes', while warm tears fell on the colourless cheeks of his father.

A gleam shone in the old man's eyes, the morning cloud stood close over him, and then the gleam, the morning cloud, and life with them, departed from him.

CHAPTER XXXI

A Long Awaited Reunion

A FEW days afterwards, Sintram stood in the parlour of
the convent and waited, with a beating heart, for his
mother to appear. He had seen her for the last time when,
a slumbering child, he had been awakened by her warm
farewell kisses, and then had fallen asleep again, to
wonder in his dreams what his mother had wanted with
him, and to seek her in vain the next morning in the
castle and in the garden.

The Chaplain was now at his side, rejoicing in the
chastened rapture of the knight, whose fierce spirit had
softened, on whose cheeks a light reflection of that solemn
morning cloud yet lingered.

The inner doors opened and, in her white veil,
stately and noble, the Lady Verena came forward, and
with a heavenly smile, she beckoned her son to approach
the grating. There could be no thought here of any
passionate outbreak, whether of sorrow or of joy.[12] The
holy peace, which had its abode within these walls, would
have found its way to a heart less tried and less purified

than that which beat in Sintram's bosom.

Shedding some placid tears, the son knelt before his mother, kissed her flowing garments through the grating, and felt as if in paradise, where every wish and every care is hushed.

"Beloved mother," said he, "let me become a holy man, as you are a holy woman. Then I will take myself to the cloister beyond, and perhaps I might one day be deemed worthy to be your confessor, if illness or the weakness of old age should keep the good Chaplain within the Castle of Drontheim."

"That would be a sweet quietly happy life, my good child," replied the Lady Verena, "but such is not your vocation. You must remain a bold powerful knight, and you must spend the long life, which is almost always granted to us children of the North, in assisting the weak, in keeping down the lawless, and in yet another more bright and honourable employment which I, up to now, rather honour than know."

"God's will be done!" said the knight, and he rose up, full of self-devotion and firmness.

"That is my good son," said the Lady Verena. "Ah! How many sweet calm joys spring up for us! See, already is our longing desire of meeting again satisfied, and you will never more be so entirely estranged from me. Every week on this day you will come back to me, and you will relate what glorious deeds you have done, and take back with you my advice and my blessing."

"Am I not once more a good and happy child!" cried Sintram joyously. "Only that the merciful God has given me, in addition, the strength of a man in body and spirit. Oh, how blessed is that son to whom it is allowed to gladden his mother's heart with the blossoms and the fruit of his life!"

Thus, he left the quiet cloister's shade, joyful in spirit and richly laden with blessings, to enter on his noble career. He was not content with going about wherever there might be a rightful cause to defend or evil to avert; the gates of the now hospitable castle stood always open also to receive and shelter every stranger; and old Rolf, who was almost grown young again at the sight of his Lord's excellence, was established as Seneschal[13].

The winter of Sintram's life set in bright and glorious, and it was only at times that he would sigh within himself and say, "Ah, Montfaucon! Ah, Gabrielle! If I could dare to hope that you have quite forgiven me!"

CHAPTER XXXII

Fulfilment of a Prophecy

THE spring had come in its brightness to the northern lands, when one morning Sintram turned his horse homewards, after a successful encounter with one of the most formidable disturbers of the peace of his neighbourhood. His horsemen rode after him, singing as they went.

As they drew near the castle, they heard the sound of joyous notes wound on the horn. "Some welcome visitor must have arrived," said the knight; and he spurred his horse to a quicker pace over the dewy meadow.

While still at some distance, they discerned old Rolf, busily engaged in preparing a table for the morning meal, under the trees in front of the castle-gates. From all the turrets and battlements, banners and flags floated in the fresh morning breeze, and esquires were running back and forth in their brightest apparel.

As soon as the good Rolf saw his master, he clapped his hands joyfully over his grey head, and hastened into the castle. Immediately the wide gates were thrown open, and as he entered, Sintram was met by Rolf, whose eyes were filled with tears of joy while he pointed towards three noble forms that were following him.

Two men of high stature – one in extreme old age, the other grey-headed, and both remarkably alike – were leading between them a fair young boy, in a page's dress of blue velvet, richly embroidered with gold. The two old men wore the dark velvet dress of German burghers, and had massive gold chains and large shining medals hanging round their necks.

Sintram had never before seen his honoured guests, and yet he felt as if they were well-known and valued friends. The very aged man reminded him of his dying father's words about the snow-covered mountains lit up by the evening sun; and then he remembered, he could scarcely tell how, that he had heard Folko say that one of the highest mountains of that sort in his southern land was called the St. Gotthard. At the same time, he knew that the old but vigorous man on the other side was named Rudlieb.

Nevertheless, the boy who stood between them, Sintram's humility dared scarcely form a hope as to who he might be, however much his features, so noble and soft, called up two highly honoured images before his mind.

Then the aged Gotthard Lenz, the king of old men, advanced with a solemn step, and said, "This is the noble boy Engeltram of Montfaucon, the only son of the great Baron. His father and mother send him to you, Sir Sintram, knowing well your holy and glorious knightly career, that you may bring him up to all the honourable and valiant deeds of this northern land, and may make of him a Christian knight, like yourself."

Sintram threw himself from his horse. Engeltram of Montfaucon held the stirrup gracefully for him, checking the retainers, who pressed forward, with these words, "I am the noblest born esquire of this knight, and the service nearest to his person belongs to me."

Sintram knelt in silent prayer on the turf; then lifting up in his arms, towards the rising sun, the image of Folko and Gabrielle, he cried, "With the help of God, my Engeltram, you will become as glorious as that sun, and your course will be like his!"

And old Rolf exclaimed, as he wept for joy, "Lord, now let Your servant depart in peace."

Gotthard Lenz and Rudlieb were pressed to Sintram's heart, and the Chaplain of Drontheim, who just then came from Verena's cloister to bring a joyful greeting to her brave son, stretched out his hands to bless them all.

NOTES

1   (p. 2) *roundelay* – a slow medieval dance performed in a circle

2   (p. 31) *cognisance* – [in heraldry] a distinguishing badge

3   (p. 32) *shawms* – medieval form of the oboe with conical bore and flaring bell, blown through a double reed

4   (p. 32) *rebecks* – medieval stringed instrument resembling the violin but having a lute-shaped body

5   (p.47) *tourneys* – [in medieval history] a knightly tournament

6   (p.54) *samite* – a heavy fabric of silk, often woven with gold or silver threads, used in the Middles Ages

7   (p.57) *Hekla* – one of Iceland's most active volcanoes, called the 'Gateway to Hell' by Europeans in the Middle Ages

8   (p.68) *girded* – to endow with a rank, especially knighthood

9   (p.100) *'Mountjoy St. Denys!'* was the war-cry of the French [*Montjoie St. Denis*]

10   (p. 109) *Castellan* – the keeper of a castle

11   (p. 136) *bark* [or *barque*] – any boat, esp. a small sailing vessel

12   (p. 166) *There could be no thought here of any passionate outbreak, whether of sorrow or of joy* – [original footnote] "In whose sweet presence sorrow dares not lower, / Nor expectation rise / Too high for earth;" excerpt from *Forms of Prayer to be Used at Sea* by John Keble, from 'Christian Year'.

13   (p. 168) *Seneschal* – steward of the household of a medieval prince or nobleman

RACHEL LOUISE LAWRENCE

British author who translates and adapts folklore and fairytales from original texts and puts them back into print.

Since writing her first story at the age of six, Rachel has never lost her love of writing and reading. A keen wildlife photographer and gardener, she is currently working on several writing projects.

Why not follow her?

 /Rachel.Louise.Lawrence

 @RLLawrenceBP

 /RLLawrenceBP

 /RachelLouiseLawrence

OTHER TITLES AVAILABLE

Madame de Villeneuve's
The Story of the Beauty and the Beast
The Original Classic French Fairytale

By Gabrielle-Suzanne Barbot de Villeneuve, Translated by James Robinson Planché, Adapted by Rachel Louise Lawrence

Think you know the story of 'Beauty and the Beast'? Think again! This book contains the original tale by Madame de Villeneuve, first published in 1740, and although the classic elements of Beauty giving up her freedom to live with the Beast, during which time she begins to see beyond his grotesque appearance, are present, there is a wealth of rich back story to how the Prince became cursed and revelations about Beauty's parentage, which fail to appear in subsequent versions. If you want to read the full story of Beauty and the Beast, look no further than this latest unabridged edition ...

ISBN-13: 978-1502992970

Sara Crewe – The Little Princess
Three-Act Playscript of the Classic Novel

By Frances Hodgson Burnett, Stageplay by Rachel Louise Lawrence

Raised in India by her affluent and adoring father, Captain Ralph Crewe, Sara was sent to London to be educated at 'Miss Minchin's Seminary for Young Ladies' at the age of seven. Impressed by Captain Crewe's fortune, and wishing to keep Sara at the school as long as possible, Miss Minchin allows Sara luxuries far beyond those of her other parlour boarders - that is until the day of Sara's eleventh birthday when Sara receives the devastating news of her adored father's death. Suddenly penniless, Miss Minchin banishes Sara to the garret to work as a servant alongside Becky, the seminary's young scullery maid. Though starved and abused, Sara uses imagination and friendship - with Becky, Ermengarde, and Lottie - to make the best of her change in situation and fortunes. However, hope is on the horizon, in the guise of a monkey and his mysterious owner who lives next door ...

ISBN-13: 978-1503282421

E-BOOK ORIGINAL TITLES AVAILABLE

Assipattle and the Mester Stoorworm
The Classic Scotland Legend

Cendrillon and the Glass Slipper
The Classic French 'Cinderella' Fairytale

East of the Sun and West of the Moon
A Norwegian Folktale

Gold-Tree and Silver-Tree
The Scottish 'Snow White' Fairytale

Irish Cinder Lad Tales
'Billy Beg and his Bull' and 'The Bracket Bull'

Persinette, The Maiden in the Tower
The Classic French 'Rapunzel' Fairytale

Snow White (First Edition)
The Original Brothers Grimm Fairytale

Talia, The Sleeping Beauty
A European Fairytale

The Singing, Springing Lark (First Edition)
The Original Brothers Grimm 'Beauty & the Beast'
Fairytale

The Story of Tom Tit Tot
The Classic English 'Rumpelstiltskin' Folktale

Zezolla, The Cat Cinderella
An Italian Fairytale

Manufactured by Amazon.ca
Bolton, ON

13875939R00107